She didn't  **...itta's**
had beco...

When Ryan s... ...itta's head was turned toward the window, and a shaft of sunlight shone on her platinum hair. His fingers itched, remembering the silkiness of those strands.

She didn't remember him. Somehow her mind had erased the last seven months. That meant she didn't remember the shooting she'd witnessed. She had no memory of being a material witness, living her life before the trial in a safe house with him as her handler.

And she definitely didn't remember that because their relationship had once been far more than FBI agent and witness, he'd had to let her go.

Or that it had killed him to do so...

CARLA CASSIDY

WITH THE
MATERIAL
WITNESS
IN THE
SAFEHOUSE

HARLEQUIN®

TORONTO • NEW YORK • LONDON
AMSTERDAM • PARIS • SYDNEY • HAMBURG
STOCKHOLM • ATHENS • TOKYO • MILAN • MADRID
PRAGUE • WARSAW • BUDAPEST • AUCKLAND

Special thanks and acknowledgment to Carla Cassidy for her contribution to the Curse of Raven's Cliff miniseries.

ISBN-13: 978-0-373-69329-0
ISBN-10:   0-373-69329-X

WITH THE MATERIAL WITNESS IN THE SAFEHOUSE

ABOUT THE AUTHOR

Carla Cassidy is an award-winning author who has written more than fifty novels for Silhouette Books. In 1995, she won Best Silhouette Romance from *Romantic Times BOOKreviews* for her novel *Anything for Danny*. In 1998, she also won a Career Achievement Award for Best Innovative Series from *Romantic Times BOOKreviews*.

Carla believes the only thing better than curling up with a good book to read is sitting down at the computer with a good story to write. She's looking forward to writing many more books and bringing hours of pleasure to readers.

Books by Carla Cassidy

Don't miss any of our special offers. Write to us at the following address for information on our newest releases.

Harlequin Reader Service
U.S.: 3010 Walden Ave., P.O. Box 1325, Buffalo, NY 14269
Canadian: P.O. Box 609, Fort Erie, Ont. L2A 5X3

CAST OF CHARACTERS

Britta Jakobsen—She was missing for days and now suffers from amnesia. Is there something in the beautiful blonde's hidden memory worth murder?

Ryan Burton—The FBI agent isn't sure he wants Britta to get her memories back.

Captain Claybourne—Does the fisherman know more than he's telling about Britta's disappearance?

Mayor Perry Wells—A grieving father who raises suspicions with his unusual actions.

Hazel Baker—She senses the evil enveloping the town. Is she a part of that evil?

Michael Kelly—Why did he bring Britta to the strange fishing village of Raven's Cliff?

Camille Wells—She was blown off the bluff on her wedding day and remains lost at sea.

Grant Bridges—His fiancée Camille disappeared on their wedding day. What is his connection?

Patrick Swanson—The chief of police knows all too well about the curse on his small town.

Chapter One

Happy is the bride that the sun shines on. If that was the case, then Camille Wells was going to be one unhappy bride, Ryan Burton thought as he stood among a huge crowd of people gathered on the rocky bluffs of Raven's Cliff, Maine.

The dismal gray sky seemed to plunge right down to the frothing water of the coastline below. A stiff breeze blew everyone's hair askew and the female guests held on to their skirts.

Beneath the hum of conversation among the attendees was the ever-present thunder of the waves crashing against the rocky shoreline. Despite the fact that it was early May the air held an oppressive closeness broken only by wind gusts, which had been strong enough to decimate the floral arrangements long ago.

Ryan had arrived in the small fishing village that morning with a specific job to accomplish, and that job had nothing to do with attending some fancy wedding ceremony. But when he'd discovered it was the mayor's daughter getting married, and everyone who was anyone would be there, he'd wrangled an invite from the innkeeper when he'd checked in.

Maybe somebody here knew something about *her* disappearance. Ryan tried to ignore the tension that knotted in his chest as he thought of the woman he'd come here to find.

Britta Jakobsen was supposed to have begun work as a housekeeper at the inn four days ago. According to the innkeeper, Hazel Baker, Britta had checked in and gone to her room and hadn't been seen since.

Later today he was to speak with Michael Kelly, the FBI agent in charge of relocating Britta here. To the FBI, Britta Jakobsen was a witness who had fingered a number of bad guys who'd been in a shoot-out that had taken place in Boston six months before.

The shoot-out had not only involved local thugs but also police and FBI agents. It had resulted in the death of one of their own, and the FBI had leaned hard on Britta for her cooperation.

There had already been one attempt on her life, resulting in her being placed in the Witness Protection Program and relocated to this small Maine fishing village.

And now she was missing.

"Ugly day for a wedding." The deep voice brought Ryan out of his thoughts.

He looked at the barrel-chested bald man standing next to him and nodded. "I've definitely seen better." As if to punctuate his sentence, a fierce wind gust nearly blew him back a step, and the scent of brine became stronger.

"Don't believe I've seen you around these parts before." The man's hazel eyes held both a wealth of intelligence and more than a touch of curiosity. "Friend of the bride or the groom?"

"Neither," Ryan admitted. "I checked into the inn this morning and Hazel invited me to come out for the wedding. She mentioned these bluffs are the best place to get a look at that." He pointed to the old lighthouse that rose up in the distance. "Hazel told me it's the stuff of local legends."

The well-built man offered a small smile. "Hazel is our resident kook. Don't let her fill your head with nonsense. Is that a touch of Texas I hear in your voice?"

Ryan eyed him in surprise. "It is. Born and raised there."

The man held out a hand. "I'm Patrick Swanson, Chief of Police."

Ryan wasn't surprised. The man definitely had the aura of power and authority. He took the proffered hand, and the two men shook. "Ryan Burton, nice to meet you."

"So, what brings you to Raven's Cliff, Ryan Burton?"

Ryan couldn't very well tell him he was in town undercover to find an important material witness who had gone missing. The last thing they wanted was any kind of publicity. "I've heard the fishing is good in these parts."

He wasn't sure yet how to handle things with the authorities here in Raven's Cliff. He'd had to tell Hazel that he'd come to look for Britta because Britta had gone missing from the inn. He was banking on the hope that Hazel wouldn't want anyone to know that a woman had disappeared from the inn under strange circumstances. It wasn't good for publicity.

"The locals are pulling in record breakers lately. I've never seen fish so big," Patrick replied.

Ryan nodded absently and gazed around at the group, wondering who among the guests might know something about the woman he sought. Again a fist knotted in the pit of his stomach. To the FBI Britta was a material witness, but to him, she had once been far more.

He focused back on Patrick, who was pointing out the town notables to him. There was Mayor Perry Wells and his wife, Beatrice, and standing nearby was Rick Simpson, the mayoral aide.

The prospective groom, Grant Bridges, was also the assistant district attorney and stood impatiently at the altar that had been set up precariously close to the edge of the bluff.

"I'm going to see if I can find out what's holding up the ceremony," Patrick said. With a nod he left Ryan standing alone.

This was probably a waste of time, Ryan thought. He'd tried to question several people immediately upon arriving in town, but the one thing he'd discovered fairly quickly was that despite the fact that part of the town's revenue came from tourism, the people of Raven's Cliff didn't appear to take too kindly to strangers.

What he hoped was that following the wedding there would be a surplus of champagne served and that would loosen lips. Somebody had to have seen Britta. A pretty blond woman like her drew attention. Somebody had to have seen or heard something that would give him a clue as to what had happened to her.

His gaze fell on the mayor, who worked the crowd with ease. Tall, with salt-and-pepper hair, the man had the polish and style of power. As Ryan watched, Mayor Wells shook a man's hand and Ryan saw a wad of money being exchanged.

He frowned. He wouldn't have found it odd if it had been the mayor passing some bills to somebody involved in the wedding, but it had been the mayor receiving the bills, not handing them out. The minute the money hit the mayor's hand, it disappeared into his pocket.

At that moment Hazel stepped up beside him. "Isn't this exciting?" she asked. Her bright yellow and orange dress threatened to balloon up, but she held it down with slightly chubby hands. "Have you found anyone who has seen Valerie?" she asked.

Britta had come to Raven's Cliff four days ago under the name of Valerie King. "Not yet, but I'm still hopeful."

"A woman as pretty as her might have caught the eye of one of our local fishermen. Maybe he reeled her right into a love nest," Hazel exclaimed, her eyes softening with a streak of obvious romanticism.

The idea of Britta in love with anyone sent a stab of pain through him. But he knew he had no right to her, and he certainly preferred she be holed up in a love nest than all the other grim possibilities that marched through his head.

"Have you talked to Captain Swanson? He's the chief of police and maybe he could help." Her plump features turned into a frown. "Maybe I should have contacted him when she didn't show up for work the morning after she checked in."

"I'm sure that's not necessary. If I know Valerie, it's just as you said, she's probably found some guy and thinks she's in love," he replied. The last thing he wanted was the local authorities involved in the case.

"She do that a lot?"

"Often enough," Ryan replied. Of course, it was a lie. Britta wasn't the type to just take off with a man or for any other reason, which was why a feeling of disquiet swept through him.

He didn't understand why Agent Kelly had chosen this particular place to relocate Britta. Strangers stuck out in small towns, even places that catered to tourists. A beautiful woman moving to town was noted.

"Oh, they're finally getting started," Hazel exclaimed as music began to swell in the air and a hush of expectancy fell over the crowd. "You know Grant sold his house and is staying at the inn right now. The mayor is giving his daughter and Grant a huge house as a wedding gift."

Hazel said no more as the mayor appeared with his daughter and began the traditional walk toward the altar. "Doesn't she look beautiful?"

Ryan murmured in agreement. The bride did look pretty in her silk and pearl gown. Burnished gold corkscrew curls fell to her shoulders and a soft smile curved the corners of her lips as she looked at Grant, waiting at the altar.

Yes, she was pretty, but Ryan's head was filled with the vision of a tall, long-legged blonde with ice-blue eyes. *Where are you, Britta?* She hadn't just disappeared into thin air.

It was a good thing the wedding was getting underway, for the weather seemed to be contemplating a turn for the worse. The skies had darkened into an ominous color of gray, and the thundering of the waves against the rocky bluffs grew louder.

It was obvious a storm was approaching. They'd have to hurry to get the vows in before nature released all its fury. The beautiful bride and her father approached the altar, and Mayor Wells did the traditional handing over of the bride to her groom.

Grant Bridges reached for Camille's hand, but at that moment a gale-force wind tore across the top of the bluff. It moved Ryan forward a step, and the bride reached up to grab her veil.

Everything appeared to happen in slow motion. As Camille reached a slender hand up to hold on to her veil she took a step backward and stumbled. Her mouth opened in surprise as her feet found no purchase.

Grant lunged out for her and desperately grabbed at the sleeve of her dress. For an instant Ryan thought he had her, but then the sleeve tore in Grant's hand, and with a small cry she tumbled off the bluff and disappeared from sight.

Stunned silence lasted only a minute, and then the crowd erupted with screams and shouts. "It's the curse," Hazel wailed. "Captain Raven's curse has struck again."

Ryan ignored her and raced to the altar, along with the mayor, Captain Swanson and half a dozen other men. Ryan lay on his stomach and eased up to the edge of the bluffs, looking over to the treacherous rocks below.

He'd expected to see the broken body of Camille. But he saw nothing. Carefully he slid backward from the treacherous edge and stood with feet braced wide apart for balance, unwilling to become another victim to the wind.

Lightning slashed the black sky, and thunder boomed overhead. Bedlam reigned. Grant had collapsed and was weeping like a baby, women screamed and held on to their husbands.

"Do something," Mayor Wells said, grabbing Patrick Swanson by the arm. "We have to find her." Perry Wells's eyes were as turbulent as the sea below.

Patrick shrugged off the mayor's desperate grasp as he opened a cell phone and spoke to somebody about search and rescue.

Ryan stared up at the angry skies, still unable to believe the tragedy that had just occurred. A freak accident. Hell, it didn't get any freakier. Of course, if he listened to Hazel, it hadn't been an accident at all; rather, Camille Wells had been the tragic victim of a curse.

Exactly what curse? Ryan was grounded in reality too much to believe in such nonsense. Still, as he thought of

Camille tumbling over the bluff, probably to her death, and the fact that Britta appeared to have disappeared into thin air, he couldn't control the chill that walked up his spine, raised the hair on his arms and iced the blood in his veins.

A SEARCH-AND-RESCUE TEAM worked for hours. Ryan volunteered to be a part of the effort to find Camille. The storm moved on without rain, leaving behind a gray pall that matched the moods of the men.

Her veil. That's all that had been found so far. Fishermen in boats dotted the water looking for her body, but so far she hadn't been spotted either in the water or along the rocks and crevices of the bluff itself.

Mayor Wells was like a man possessed. He'd taken his distraught wife home, then had returned to help search for his daughter. Grant Bridges, the groom without a bride, had been sedated and taken to the local clinic.

Twilight was approaching, and Ryan knew the search would soon be called off for the night. He stood on the shore staring up at the bluff where Camille had gone over the edge. It was as if the earth had opened and swallowed her whole.

Like Britta.

He frowned. Britta wouldn't have just disappeared on her own. She knew the importance of the FBI knowing where she was. They had gone to a lot of trouble to set her up here with a new identity and a new job. She just wasn't the type to blow off all their hard work.

Had one of the men who had made an attempt on her life in Boston found her? Even though he'd walked away from her two months ago with the realization that he'd never see her again, he'd taken comfort in the fact that eventually she'd find some man to love, would build the family she wanted and live a wonderful life.

His frown deepened as his gaze swept the area, lingering on the abandoned Beacon Manor lighthouse that still showed the blackened scars of the fire that had consumed the top of the forty-foot conical building some time ago.

He froze as something caught his eye, a flash of white against the blackened beams, a ghostly wraith that was there only a moment, then gone.

If he were a superstitious man, he would have guessed that the apparition was the dead wife of Sea Captain Earl Raven seeking her husband. But Ryan was firmly grounded in reality. He didn't believe in curses or ghosts.

He rubbed a hand over tired eyes and wondered if it had been nothing more than his imagination. He supposed it was possible it might be the missing bride, although he couldn't imagine how she would have survived her fall off the bluff and be able to climb the stairs to the top of the lighthouse.

Knowing he wouldn't be satisfied until he checked it out, he left the bluffs and headed back to his car to drive the short distance to the lighthouse.

As he passed the area that had been set up as a command post for the search-and-rescue team, he caught a glimpse of the police chief. Patrick Swanson had impressed him. Ryan would guess the man to be in his sixties, and although he had the body of a man half his age, he also had the command and cool-headedness that came with wisdom.

The wind had picked up again, buffeting his car as he approached the rocky shore where the lighthouse rose up like a sand castle.

A low-lying blanket of fog had moved in, nearly obscuring the base of the structure. Maybe that's what he'd seen. A wisp of fog. No ghost, no missing bride, just a freak of nature that had momentarily looked like a person.

He'd have to hurry. Before long total darkness would descend and he'd brought no flashlight with him. Although he sensed no danger, he drew his gun from his shoulder holster.

From the moment he'd arrived in Raven's Cliff he'd felt an underlying aura of something unsettling. He'd only experienced it once before in his life in a small Louisiana bayou.

At that time they'd been chasing a schizophrenic man who had kidnapped a six-year-old girl. It had taken only minutes of being in Black Bay to realize that the townspeople appeared to have more secrets than the man they were hunting.

There had been a happy ending to that situation, and he hoped his hunt for Britta would result in the same kind of ending. With his gun held steady before him, he started up the wrought iron stairs that wound clockwise inside the stone tower.

"Haunted, it is," Hazel had said that morning. "If it's not the ghost of Captain Earl Raven's wife that haunts the place then it surely is the ghost of Nicholas Sterling who set the curse into motion."

"Ghost, my ass," Ryan muttered to himself. He counted twenty steps before he reached a small landing. He stared upward, but saw nothing, although he heard the scurry of what he assumed were mice. He heard nothing else to cause him alarm, but unexpected tension pressed hard against his chest.

Fog drifted in the broken windows, tendrils of gray smoke that added to the eerie atmosphere of the abandoned building.

He'd just reached the second landing when he heard the echo of something above him. A footfall?

He tightened his grip on the gun as he entered what he knew was the service area. At one time this room would have held all the lighthouse keeper's equipment, but now the cabinets that hung on the walls had open doors that displayed empty shelves.

Above him was the watch room, and around it would be the lookout deck. It had been there that he'd thought he'd seen somebody. He eased up the stairs, his gun leading the way.

The watch room was empty, but in the dust on the floor he saw bare footprints. Small feet, definitely not a man's. Did ghosts leave footprints? He didn't think so.

He opened the iron door that led to the deck. As he stepped outside, the evening air pressed in, thick and oppressive. The view from this observation point was breathtaking. The ocean pummeled the shore, where rocks jutted upward and glistened with deadly intent.

Directly across from where he stood was the bluff where a wedding had turned to tragedy. Although a few boats still bobbed in the water below, it looked as if the search-and-rescue operation had been called off for the night.

He whipped around as he heard a noise to his left. A gasp escaped him as he saw the woman who stood before him. It was obvious that she was naked beneath the gauzy white gown. An intricate shell necklace adorned her pale, slender neck, and her ice-blue eyes seemed to peer right through him.

"Britta," he gasped in stunned surprise.

"Have you come to take me back to the sea?" Her Norwegian accent was thicker than he'd ever heard. That fact, coupled with the otherworldly look in her eyes as she smiled at him caused a wave of horror to roar through him.

"Britta, it's me, Ryan." He quickly holstered his weapon and took a step closer to her.

"Please, sir, take me back to the sea." With a tiny sigh her eyes rolled back in her head and she collapsed at his feet.

Chapter Two

Britta dreamed of the sea, of being deep below the surface in the silence of the underworld. The warm water surrounded her, and she felt as safe, as secure as if she were a baby in her mother's womb.

However the secure feeling disappeared as the water around her became icy cold and turbulent, tossing her weightless body like a leaf in a water-swelled gutter. The water that had moments before embraced her now imprisoned her, pressing against her chest as if to squeeze the very life from her.

She looked up and saw the surface far above her, knew that she needed to get there before the sea choked the last gasp of life from her.

She struggled against the mysterious force that tried to keep her down, panic rising as she moved her arms and legs as fast, as hard as she could.

The sea wanted her. She was to be a sacrifice. The words pounded in her head, but she didn't know what they meant. She cried as she swam up...up...needing air, wanting life. When she broke the surface, she cried out.

And woke up.

For a moment panic seared through her as she realized she didn't know where she was or how she'd gotten here.

The panic didn't subside when she saw that she was in a hospital bed. Frantically she moved her arms, her legs, to make certain that everything worked all right. A touch of the terror ebbed. Everything appeared to work just fine and she was in no pain.

She turned her head toward the window where the morning sun streaked in, and stifled a small gasp as she saw a man sleeping in the chair next to the window, a newspaper on his chest.

His buzz-cut, sun-streaked brown hair glinted in the sunlight. Even in sleep his lean features looked stern and slightly dangerous. His face had character lines that let her know he wasn't a young man, probably in his thirties.

Who was he? Why was he here in her hospital room? And why was she in a hospital?

A new panic gripped her as she tried to remember what had happened the day before. Had she been in a car accident? Had she taken a bad fall?

She tried to remember, desperately wanted to remember, but there was nothing. Her mind was a blank slate. The last memory she had was going into her office at the hotel to take care of some paperwork.

Her job. Whatever had happened to her that had put her here, she hoped it hadn't jeopardized her job as an assistant manager for the upscale Boston hotel, the Woodlands. The job had been a real coup for her after finishing her degree in hotel management.

At that moment the man's eyes snapped opened. "Britta." Earthy green eyes stared at her as he stood and approached the side of her bed. "You're awake," he said, stating the obvious. "How are you feeling?"

She clutched the sheet more tightly against her chest. "Okay, I guess. Who are you?"

A deep frown ripped across his tanned forehead. "You don't recognize me?" He stepped closer to the side of the bed.

He had a wonderful voice, deep and resonating with the hint of a cowboy accent. But, there was nothing cowboy about him. His black slacks clung to long, lean legs and his short-sleeved white shirt exposed strong arm muscles and stretched across his broad shoulders.

His expression told her she should recognize him. Perhaps he was a hotel guest that she'd met. "I'm sorry, I don't remember. Have we met before? Are you a guest at the hotel?"

She wouldn't have thought it possible for his frown to deepen, but it did. His eyes searched her features for so long she grew even more anxious.

"My name is Ryan Burton." He took yet another step closer to her and she smelled the scent of him, a clean masculine scent with a hint of spice. It was oddly familiar. "Are you sure you don't recognize me?"

"I'm sorry. I…did I hit my head? Is that why I'm here?" It was her turn to frown. Why, oh, why couldn't she remember?

"Do you know what day it is?"

"Of course," she replied, and then frowned again thoughtfully. She remembered specifically that yesterday had been October 30. The hotel had been bedecked with fall decorations, and a Halloween gala had been planned for the next evening. She'd been in charge of the festivities, and her boss had been pleased with her arrangements.

"Today is Halloween," she finally said.

His expression radiated shock. "I'm going to go get your doctor and let him know you're conscious. I'll be right back."

When he left the room, Britta slid her legs over the side of the bed, surprised by the general weakness that gripped her body. She drew a deep breath.

It had been obvious from Ryan's face when she'd told him the date that she'd been wrong. The newspaper that he'd set on the chair when he'd gotten up should tell her how far off she'd been. Maybe she'd been unconscious for longer than a day.

She was shocked to find herself completely naked beneath the blue floral hospital gown. She clutched the back of the garment closed as she rose unsteadily to her feet.

I'm as weak as a baby, she thought as she reached the chair and grabbed the newspaper. She clutched it to her chest and returned to the safety of the bed. Drawing another deep breath, exhausted by the short foray, she pushed the button that would raise the head of the bed, then opened the newspaper.

Raven's Cliff Daily News. The bold black letters marched around the top of the paper. Raven's Cliff? Where was that? She'd never heard of such a place.

The headline screamed in even bigger letters. Tragedy on Raven's Cliff bluff—Bride Still Missing. She scanned the story quickly, shocked to read that a bride-to-be had fallen off some sort of bluff just moments before exchanging her wedding vows.

She glanced at the tiny print beneath the name of the paper, a startled gasp escaping her as she read the date, May 3.

May? How was that possible? The last thing she remembered was a day in October. Where had the months gone and why couldn't she remember?

Maybe the newspaper was fake, one of those silly ones people could pay to have printed up. But why would somebody print up a paper detailing the tragedy of a bride falling off a cliff? Or maybe it was a paper from last May.

Frantic, she looked up as the man named Ryan and another tall blonde in a doctor's coat entered the room. "Is this true?" she asked. "Is the date May third?"

"Hi, I'm Dr. Jamison." The doctor pulled up the chair next to her bed and sat. "And yes, the date today is May third. What date did you think it was?"

Britta was afraid to answer, knowing that her reply would let the doctor know just how messed up she really was. "Halloween," she said in a faint voice. "The last day that I remember was the day before Halloween."

A wrinkle raced across Dr. Jamison's forehead. "Can you tell me your name?"

"Of course. Britta Jakobsen. Now, please, tell me what's happened. Why am I in the hospital? Have I been sick? Maybe in a coma?" That would explain the missing time.

"Last night I found you wandering the old lighthouse here in town. You were dressed in a white gown and were wearing a seashell necklace," Ryan said. "You fainted and I brought you here."

His words did nothing to alleviate the fear and confusion in her head. Wandering a lighthouse? What on earth was going on? "And where, exactly is here?"

"Raven's Cliff Clinic," the doctor replied. "In Raven's Cliff, Maine."

Maine? What was she doing here? She'd never been to Maine in her life. Her work, her apartment, everything she knew was in Boston. "Please, tell me what's happened to me?" She looked at the doctor, then at Ryan, then back again to the doctor, a frantic panic surging up inside her.

Dr. Jamison frowned and reached out for her hand. She'd thought he'd meant to offer comfort, but instead he placed his fingertips against her rapidly beating pulse. "I can't tell you what's happened to bring you here, but I can tell you that your vital signs are all good. The tests we've run on you show no indication of trauma or illness. However, an initial toxicology screen showed something interesting."

"Interesting how?" Ryan asked and took a step closer, and once again Britta was struck by the fact that the clean, but subtle spicy scent of his cologne seemed intimately familiar to her.

She wondered in the back of her mind how well they had known each other? But she couldn't think about that right now. There were other, more-pressing issues to be concerned about, like what had happened to her and how she'd ended up in Raven's Cliff, Maine.

The doctor looked at Ryan, then back at her. "There's a privacy issue involved here. Would you prefer that Mr. Burton leave the room while I speak with you about your condition?"

Britta had no idea who Ryan Burton was and why he had apparently spent the night in her room, but the idea of him leaving her all alone scared her almost as much as anything the doctor might say to her.

"No. Whatever you have to say you can speak freely with Mr. Burton here," she replied. Privacy be damned, she didn't want to be alone.

Dr. Jamison released her hand and sat back in his chair. "I found traces in your system of a new designer drug that's springing up in the area. I believe the street name for it is Stinging Flower."

"That's impossible," Britta exclaimed. "I don't take drugs."

"There were three fresh injection sites on your thigh," Dr. Jamison said. "If you didn't willingly take it, then somebody gave it to you."

"What is it? What does it do?" Ryan asked.

The world seemed to tilt on its axis for Britta. She'd lost seven months of her life, was in a town where she didn't belong and had been injected with some kind of new drug. Tears pressed hotly at her eyes, but she swallowed against them, refusing to allow either man to see her cry.

"We don't know a lot about it yet. All we know for sure is that the drug contains a derivative of the stinging cells of the anemone."

"What's an anemone?" Britta asked. She reached up and twisted a finger in a strand of her hair, the rhythmic motion somewhat calming.

"They're sea animals that usually live on rocks and in the sand and look like flowers," Dr. Jamison explained. "They're armed with a toxin that paralyzes their prey, and it seems some illustrious person has managed to get those toxins into a new street drug."

"But she wasn't paralyzed when I found her," Ryan protested. "She was walking around, although it was like she was in a daze."

"Apparently, the street drug has a number of other components to it and one of the effects is that while it doesn't paralyze, it does put the person under the influence into a state of high suggestibility."

"You mean, like a hypnotic trance?" Ryan asked.

The doctor nodded and once again gazed at Britta. "And I would attribute your state of amnesia to the residual effects of the drugs combined with some sort of emotional trauma."

"Is the amnesia permanent?" She was afraid of his answer. She dropped her hand from her hair and instead clutched tightly to the sheet that covered her.

"My professional opinion is I don't know." He offered her a smile of apology. "My personal opinion is that probably not. I think if you give your body and your mind some time to rest, time to recover, eventually your memory will probably return. Even though we're a small clinic with limited resources, I'd like to keep you here under observation for another twenty-four hours."

She wanted to protest, but then she remembered how weak she'd been when she'd left the bed to retrieve the newspaper. She nodded her assent reluctantly and then added, "But I need to make some phone calls, to check on my job and see what's happened with my apartment."

"I'll leave you two alone for now." Dr. Jamison stood and smiled at Britta. "I'll have somebody bring you in a breakfast tray."

"I'm really not hungry," she protested.

Dr. Jamison shot her a sympathetic look as he headed for the door, then stopped and wagged a finger at her. "You have to eat. It's important that you take care of yourself."

Ryan followed the doctor to the door. "I'm going to have a chat with Dr. Jamison, then we need to have a long talk."

There was an intensity in those lush green eyes of his that made her want to run and hide. She had a horrible feeling that the bad news wasn't finished yet.

"YOU KNOW her name isn't Britta," Ryan told the doctor as the two men walked down the hallway. It was imperative that Ryan guard her real identity, so when he'd brought her in he'd checked her in as Valerie King. "Her name is Valerie King, and she isn't from Boston but Chicago."

Dr. Jamison frowned. "Then it's possible she's suffering some false memory issue from the drug. What's your relationship to her?"

"A close personal friend. She doesn't have any family. I'm all she has. Four days ago she was supposed to call me when she got settled here in Raven's Cliff. When she didn't call and I couldn't get in touch with her, I decided to come and see what was going on. I arrived yesterday in town just in time to help with the search for Camille Wells."

Dr. Jamison grimaced and shook his head. "Terrible tragedy. Last I heard they haven't found her body yet. The mayor and his wife are absolutely beside themselves with grief."

Ryan remembered that brief moment when he'd seen money pass between the mayor and another man. It had struck him as being odd at the time. There had been something covert about the exchange, but in the wake of Camille's stumble off the bluff, it had been forgotten until this moment.

Even now he wasted no time or thought on the mayor or the tragic wedding ceremony. "There's nothing more you can do for Valerie? Nothing to help with the amnesia?"

"I think she's suffering a temporary fugue state, but I can't give you any real prognosis. The brain is a complicated thing. Add in a drug that we know little about and don't know how to counteract, and there's not much we can do."

"You've seen this drug before?"

"Only twice." Dr. Jamison glanced at his watch, then looked back at Ryan. "Both times the victims, if you will, were college girls who had been at keg parties. They were brought in by friends who got scared." He shook his head. "Booze and stupidity are a dangerous combination."

"Valerie is neither a drinker nor stupid," Ryan replied. "I would appreciate it if you wouldn't release any information about her being here or anything else about her condition. Until we know what's happened to her and who might be responsible, I'd prefer nobody know she's been found and under what circumstances."

"I would have no reason to release any information, and I'll make sure my nurse understands that, as well." Dr. Jamison glanced at his watch once again. "I'm sorry, I've got other patients waiting. I'll check in with you later this afternoon."

Ryan watched the doctor walk down the hallway, then pulled a cell phone from his pocket. He had arrangements to make for Britta. He had no idea what had happened to her, who had drugged her, but her safety was paramount.

With the phone call made and plans in progress, he walked back toward Britta's room, dreading the conversation he was about to have with her.

When he stepped back into the room, her head was turned toward the window and a shaft of sunlight shone on her platinum hair. His fingers itched, remembering the silkiness of those strands.

She didn't remember him. Somehow her mind had erased the past seven months. That meant she didn't remember the shooting she'd witnessed. She had no memory of being a material witness, living her life before the trial in a safehouse with him as her handler.

She didn't remember that their relationship had become far more than FBI agent and witness. She didn't remember that they had become lovers.

She turned her head then, as if sensing his presence as he entered the room. "You doing okay?" he asked.

"Of course I'm not," she replied with a slight edge to her voice.

"You haven't touched your breakfast," he said, noting the tray that had apparently been delivered while he was speaking to Dr. Jamison.

"I can't eat. My head aches from trying to figure out what's happened to me in the past seven months." She reached up and grabbed a strand of her hair, twisting it around her finger in what he knew was a nervous gesture.

Ryan sat in the chair next to the bed. "I can help fill in some of those blanks for you." He tried to figure out the kindest way to tell her of the path her life had taken since the night she last remembered, and decided a direct approach was best. "There is no job for you to worry about back in Boston," he said. "Nor is there an apartment for you to return to."

She stared at him as if he'd spoken a foreign language. A pulse beat along the side of her neck and he remembered exactly what her skin tasted like there. It was an unwanted memory that he consciously shoved away.

"Tell me," she demanded, and pulled her hand from her hair. "Tell me what happened. What I remember is that my life was on track, that I'd landed the job I'd dreamed of and my future looked bright. What happened to bring me here?"

Her Norwegian accent came through strong again, a sure sign of the stress she was under. "What you remember is right, but the night before Halloween all of that changed. That night you witnessed a shoot-out between several FBI agents and members of a sophisticated but deadly street gang. One of our agents died that night, and you were instrumental in testifying against some of the guilty parties." He paused to allow her time to digest what he'd told her so far.

"So you're an FBI agent?"

He nodded. "And I was your personal handler, the man who was assigned to keep you safe between the time of the shooting and the trial. Despite one attempt on your life, we managed to get you safely through the process, but because several of the gang members who were still out on the streets had promised retribution, we encouraged you to enter the Witness Protection Program."

She raised a trembling hand to tuck a strand of her hair behind her ear and once again gazed out the window. Ryan remained silent, unwilling to give her more information until she indicated she was ready for more.

She finally turned to face him once again, her blue eyes glinting with the strength he'd come to admire in her during the time they'd been together. "So, how did I come to be here in Raven's Cliff?"

"This was to be your new home. Your new identity was of Valerie King, a twenty-six-year-old woman from Chicago. You arrived here in Raven's Cliff Tuesday and were supposed to begin work as a housekeeper in the local inn on Wednesday morning. Your current handler, Michael Kelly, tried to call you, and when he couldn't get an answer and you didn't return his calls, he informed me that we might have lost you."

"So you came here from Boston to find me?" she asked. He nodded.

"Kelly was in the middle of another assignment and couldn't get away."

"And you found me at the top of a lighthouse." She

rubbed dainty fingers across the center of her forehead, as if in an attempt to ease a headache. "So, what happens now?"

"I've arranged to take you to a safehouse when you're released tomorrow."

Her eyes, always a window to her thoughts, displayed a hint of distrust. "How do I know you are who you say you are? How do I know that anything you're telling me is true?"

Her questions pleased him. They proved to him that, despite the amnesia, her brain was working well. He grabbed his wallet from his pants and pulled out his official Bureau identification. "I'll get some documentation to bring to you later this afternoon that will support everything I've told you."

She handed the identification back to him, her gaze holding his intently. "I'm afraid." The words were just a whisper. "I feel so alone. Can I trust you, Ryan Burton?"

"With your very life," he replied.

She drew a deep breath. "I'm tired now. I think I'll take a nap."

"I'll be back later this afternoon." He stood and wished he could take the fear out of her eyes, pull her into his arms and assure her everything was going to be all right. Instead he murmured a goodbye and left the room.

He'd just stepped out of the clinic when his cell phone rang. His caller identification indicated it was Michael Kelly.

"How is she?" Kelly asked.

"Physically she appears to be okay but she's suffering from amnesia."

"Amnesia? You mean, like she doesn't know who she is?"

Ryan headed to his rental car. "She knows who she is, but she doesn't remember the shooting, the trial or anything else that's happened in the past seven months of her life."

"Wow. So, she can't tell you where she's been for the past four days?"

"She has no clue." Ryan reached his car and got inside.

"Is this amnesia permanent?"

"The doctor doesn't know. He thinks it might have been tied to a drug she was apparently given."

"You need me to come out there?" Kelly asked.

"Not right now. At the moment she's still in the clinic. What I do need you to do is see what you can find out about a new designer drug, street name Stinging Flower."

"Stinging Flower. Got it," Kelly replied. "What are your plans?"

"I'm getting Britta settled into a safehouse here in town." Ryan tightened his grip on the cell phone. "Then I'm going to do a little investigating and see what I can find out about where she's been for the last four days and who administered the drug to her. Something isn't right here in Raven's Cliff. I feel it in my bones."

"You'll keep me informed?" Kelly asked.

"Of course," Ryan replied, then the two men said their goodbyes and hung up.

Ryan sat behind the steering wheel and gazed up to the second-floor window that was Britta's clinic room. *Have you come to take me back to the sea?*

A chill walked up his spine as he thought of Britta in that gauzy white dress with the shell necklace around her neck and the blank look in her eyes. What had her words meant? Where had she been for the past four days, and who had injected her with a hypnotic drug?

When he'd first heard she was missing, he feared that a member of the gang had somehow found her and delivered on their promise of retribution. He no longer believed that. If a member of the Boston Gentlemen had found her, she'd certainly be dead.

It would have been easier if she weren't suffering from amnesia. He put his key into the ignition and started the car.

In one way the amnesia was something of a blessing. She wouldn't remember that he was the man who'd kept her safe for months, but she also wouldn't remember that he was the man who had broken her heart.

Chapter Three

"I don't understand how I can know that my parents immigrated to New England when I was thirteen years old, that my first-grade teacher's name was Mrs. Zoller and that I wore a navy blue dress to my high school prom, but I can't remember what's happened over the past seven months of my life." Britta released a sigh of frustration and twisted a strand of her hair around her index finger.

"You heard what the doctor told you—don't try to push it, and hopefully your memory will eventually return," Ryan said as he turned the steering wheel to make a left-hand turn.

She released her hair and cast him a surreptitious glance. He'd shown up this morning at the clinic with newspaper articles, clippings and official documents to substantiate everything he'd told her the day before.

She'd read about the shooting in Boston, about testifying at the trial and had finally agreed to go with him to the safehouse. She really had no other choice. She wasn't sure whom she could trust, but Ryan Burton had the right credentials and she felt as if she had little other choice.

"Where is this place you're taking me?" she asked.

"A little bungalow down by the docks."

She frowned and turned her attention out the window. The skies were overcast and the streets were still fairly deserted due to the early morning hour. The shops they passed looked quaint and inviting, but an unexpected shiver whispered up her spine. "Wouldn't it be better if we just left this place altogether?"

She didn't know whether the chill came from the knowledge that she had no memory, that she was in the company of a man she didn't know if she could trust or if it came from the gray-shrouded little fishing village itself. All she knew was she had an overwhelming desire to escape, but escape where?

Ryan shot her a quick glance, his intense green eyes giving nothing away of his inner thoughts. "We can't leave here until I know for sure where you've been and what happened to you in those missing four days."

"You're worried about the last four days of my life and I'm missing months," she replied dryly.

He pulled into the driveway of a tiny pale blue cottage with yellow trim. He parked in front of the detached garage, then unfastened his seat belt and turned to look at her once again.

"I'm not particularly worried about the months you can't remember because I know where you were and what you were doing for most of that time. But you came here and promptly disappeared. Somebody gave you a drug that has a hypnotic effect and we don't know who or, more important, why. The answers to those questions are here and we're not leaving until we have them."

She could drown in his eyes, the green depths pulling her in. She broke eye contact with him and rubbed a hand across her forehead where a headache pounded with unrelenting madness.

"Let's get settled in," he said.

Together they got out of the car and he led her to a side

door. He unlocked the door and they entered into a small kitchen. The blue and yellow colors of the exterior continued here with yellow curtains at the window and blue-and-yellow tiles on the floor.

It was a cheerful room, but the cheerfulness couldn't ease the edge of disquiet that fluttered through her. She was putting her trust in a man she couldn't remember, staying in a town where something had happened to her that she knew in her soul hadn't been good.

What's more, even though she didn't remember Ryan, just looking at him evoked an edge of something she couldn't quite identify…a tension of sorts that had nothing to do with the situation but everything to do with the man.

Wanting to explore the place she would call home for at least the next couple of days, she left the kitchen and entered into the small living room.

Once again the floor was tiled, probably because of the close proximity to the ocean and the sandy beaches. The furniture was simple, a sofa and love seat in dark beige, wooden coffee table and an entertainment unit holding a television and several ragged paperback novels.

The hallway led to a bathroom and one small bedroom with a double bed and a dresser. The walls were a cool summer green, complemented by the green-and-white spread on the bed.

"You can have this room and I'll bunk on the sofa," Ryan said from behind her.

She turned to face him. "Who owns this place?"

"A young couple who comes here for a month in the summer and rents it out the rest of the year. For the next three months the FBI has rented it."

"Three months? Surely we won't be here that long." She

felt as if she'd already lost so much of her life. She didn't want to lose another three months. But when this was all over, where would she begin her new life? She raised a hand to her head once again where her headache had intensified.

"Headache?" he asked. She gave him a small nod and thought she saw a flash of sympathy darken his eyes. "Why don't you lie down for a little while? I've got phone calls to make, and once you feel better, we'll talk about how things are going to go here."

At the moment lying down sounded like a wonderful idea. She hadn't realized how weak she still was until this moment. The bed looked inviting, and at least if she took a little nap, she wouldn't have to worry about the fact that she couldn't remember her immediate past and had no idea what her future held.

As Ryan left the bedroom, Britta stretched out on the bed. She lay on her back and stared up at the ceiling, trying to process everything she knew, but finding it impossible not to dwell on all the things she didn't know.

She wasn't even wearing her own clothes. Ryan had arrived at the clinic that morning with a bag of clothing from a nearby discount store. Although the underclothes had been the right size, the sweatpants and sweatshirt were far too big and an ugly color, not quite yellow and not quite green.

With a sigh she closed her eyes. The dream began before she realized she'd fallen asleep. She saw herself in a long white gown. An intricate necklace of seashells lay heavy around her neck.

The sand was warm beneath her feet as she walked the shore. The moon overhead was full, illuminating the tumultuous waves with a ghostly light.

The sea called to her, wanting her to come home. She walked toward the water, unable to fight the siren song that sang in her head, urging her forward.

She barely felt the salty water that embraced first her feet, then her legs, although she gasped slightly as it reached her waist and then her chest. She continued to walk until the water was up to her neck, then her chin, then finally over her head.

There was no panic, nothing except a strange calm acceptance that this was where she was supposed to be. The sea was her destiny.

It wasn't until she was deep beneath the surface where the moon no longer shone that panic first stirred in her. Her heart pounded as she realized she couldn't breathe. Her lungs began to burn and she tried to swim up, but anemones in various shapes and colors wrapped around her and held her in place. She fought, thrashing her arms and legs in an attempt to escape.

"Britta!"

The deep voice pulled her from the dream, and her eyes snapped open to see Ryan sitting on the edge of the bed. For just a moment it seemed completely natural for him to be on the bed with her, and that only added to her confusion.

He stood, every muscle in his body rigid as he shoved his hands into his pocket. "You must have been having a nightmare. You were crying out."

She sat up and tried to remember her dream, but it slipped away as full consciousness returned. "I'm sorry." She worried a hand through her hair. "How long was I asleep?"

"About an hour. How's the headache?"

"Better." She swung her legs over the side of the bed and stood.

"I fixed lunch. Are you hungry?" he asked as they left the bedroom.

She nodded, surprised to discover that she was hungry. The catered clinic food had been abysmal, so she didn't know when the last time was that she'd had a good meal.

He pointed her to a chair at the table where he'd already set plates and silverware, then went to the refrigerator and pulled out a bowl of pasta salad. He set it in the middle of the table, then returned to the fridge for a platter of cold cuts. "It's nothing elaborate."

"It looks good."

He handed her a bottle of diet soda, then poured himself a glass of milk. It was disconcerting that he knew her well enough to know what she'd want to drink, and yet she couldn't remember a darn thing about him.

"We need to go by the inn and get my things," she said once he was settled in the chair opposite her. "I'm assuming I arrived here in town with at least a suitcase."

"I don't want to do that," he replied. "I bought you some extra clothes and I'll get you whatever else you need."

She frowned. "I don't understand. Why can't I just get my own things?" Maybe the familiarity of her own clothes would jog something in her memory.

"Right now the only person who knows that you've been found is the doctor and a nurse or two. I don't want anyone else to know because I intend to ask questions about you, questions that will hopefully make somebody nervous enough to show themselves."

"And then what?"

"Then we find out just what in the hell happened to you over those four days."

An unexpected chill walked up her spine. She wasn't at all sure she wanted to know what had happened to her.

RYAN SHOULD NEVER HAVE gone into the bedroom when he'd heard her crying out. Seeing Britta lying on the bed had brought back a rush of memories he'd tried hard to forget. Even now, as he sat across the table from her, those memories of making love with her lit a simmering flame in the pit of his stomach.

She'd been a wildly passionate lover, a woman comfortable with her own body and equally comfortable with his. They'd been holed up in a duplex for months and there had been few places in that tiny space that they hadn't made love.

He cast her a surreptitious glance. She picked at the pasta salad as if finding it nearly unpalatable. "You know, if you don't like it, you don't have to eat it," he said. "I'm not exactly a master chef."

She looked up at him and smiled. It was the first smile she'd offered him, and the power of that gesture kicked him right in the stomach. "It's very good. I'm just not as hungry as I thought I was." She set down her fork, obviously deciding not even to pretend to eat.

"I'm overwhelmed at the moment by everything that's happened since I woke up in the clinic," she said softly. "I guess I'd feel more comfortable if I at least remembered you."

He'd feel more comfortable if she never remembered him. "We just need to take this one day at a time," he replied. "Hopefully in the next couple of days I can find out what happened to you, and in the meantime maybe your memory will start to come back."

"I hope so," she said fervently. She tilted her head slightly to one side and gazed at him for a long moment. "I feel as if

I'm at such a disadvantage here. You know me well enough to know what I'd want to drink with my lunch and yet I don't know anything about you."

"I know what you like to drink because while you were in my custody we ate meals together, but we didn't share a lot of personal information." He looked down at his plate so she wouldn't see the lie in his eyes.

If and when she regained her memories there would probably be hell to pay for the lies he was telling, but he'd worry about that when the time came.

"So, we weren't really friends?" There was a faint wistfulness in her tone.

He could only imagine that in her present state she was desperately seeking a connection to somebody…to anybody. "We were friendly," he conceded.

She smiled again, and the flame that had lit in the pit of his stomach burned a little hotter. He got up from the table, feeling the need to get out of there, to escape her nearness.

Besides, he had work to do, and it wouldn't get done by him sitting here with her. "I'm going to finish unloading the car, then head out for a couple of hours." He didn't wait for her reply but went out the back door and to the car.

He had not only his suitcase in the trunk, but also several shopping bags from the discount store. He gathered up everything and returned to the cottage.

Britta followed him into the living room where he dumped all the bags on the sofa. "There're clothes and toiletries for you in here." He placed his suitcase on the floor and opened it. On top of his clothes was a cell phone and charger. "This is for you," he said as he handed her the phone, then plugged the charger into an electric socket in the wall.

"I'll give you my number so that you can call me if you need me," he continued. "Stay away from the doors and windows. Nobody knows you're here and I want to keep it that way."

"So basically I'm a prisoner here," she said flatly.

He forced a lazy grin to his lips. "That's right, darlin', and I'm your number-one jailer." He laced his voice with his Texas drawl. "And while I'm out trying to figure out what's going on in this little village, you might want to use your energy and cook me up a good dinner."

Her eyes narrowed and her back went rigid, just as he knew they would. She'd hated it before when he'd used the little-woman routine on her, which was why he wanted to use it and see if it brought back any memories. The fact that she merely nodded and didn't explode let him know just how fragile she was.

"I should be back in a couple of hours." Once again he felt an incredible need to gain some distance from her. "Lock the doors and call me if you need anything."

He didn't wait for her reply but instead stepped out of the back door and into the briny-scented air. This was going to be more difficult than he'd thought.

When he'd walked away from Britta months ago, he'd put her in his past. He'd been determined never to see her again, that she would never be part of his life again. But her disappearance and the fact that she might be in trouble had changed everything.

He stood in front of the house and gathered his thoughts. He'd start at the docks. He wasn't sure of the best way to proceed, but he'd decided to play the role of Britta's boyfriend, desperately seeking any information about his missing lover.

He patted his pocket where he had a picture of himself and

Britta tucked inside. It had been taken months ago, and it was a particularly good photo of Britta.

As he headed toward the docks, dark clouds hung low overhead and the scent of decaying fish grew stronger despite a wind that had picked up. The ocean looked unwelcoming with whitecaps shooting up with tremendous force. A rumble of thunder in the distance announced a coming storm.

A group of men sat at an old wooden picnic table, their sunburned faces identifying them as men who spent most of their time on the water. Ryan ambled toward them with a friendly smile. If he was ever going to pull out his good-ol'-boy-from-Texas act, now was the time.

"How you all doing?" he asked, then cast his gaze back out to the tumultuous sea. "Guess it's not a good day to be out fishing."

"We can afford to take a day off," a man with white hair and a grizzly beard said. "Been pulling in the best hauls of our lives lately."

"Ryan Burton," Ryan said, and stuck out his hand.

"They call me Captain Claybourne," the old man said as he grabbed Ryan's hand in a firm shake. He pointed to the man next to him, a young man with a shock of blond hair. "This here is Sam Lanier." Ryan nodded, and Captain Claybourne then pointed to the man across the table. "And that's Alex Gibson." Alex Gibson raised a hand in greeting, his bright blue eyes holding a touch of reserve.

"So, the fishing business has been booming," Ryan said as Captain Claybourne gestured him to a seat at the table.

"I've been fishing these waters for fifty years, and I've never seen anything like it," Claybourne exclaimed, and shook his head. "We're pulling in new records every day. It doesn't seem to matter what kind of fish it is, they're all as big as I've ever seen them."

"Gonna make us all wealthy men," Sam said with a wide grin.

"Don't be spending the money too freely," Alex said. "You never know with the sea when things might go bad again."

There was a sober moment of silence, then Captain Claybourne eyed Ryan curiously. "You vacationing here in Raven's Cliff?"

"Actually, I'm trying to chase down a woman," Ryan replied.

"Aren't we all," Alex replied dryly.

The other two men hooted. "Don't let Lucy hear you saying stuff like that," Sam exclaimed. "Lucy owns Tidal Treasures, a little trinket shop," he explained to Ryan, "and she and Alex have been seeing each other."

"Well, I'm here in town looking for my girlfriend," Ryan replied as he pulled the photo from his pocket. He handed it to Captain Claybourne, aware of a subtle hierarchy among the men. "She got here a couple of days ago but nobody has seen her since the night she arrived."

Claybourne looked at the photo then shook his head and handed it to Sam. "Sorry, I haven't seen her around."

"Me, neither," Sam replied.

Alex took the photo and studied it, then shrugged his broad shoulders. "Sorry." He handed the photo back to Ryan, who pocketed it once again.

"Have you talked to Captain Swanson?" Claybourne asked.

"Nah, I've been reluctant to go to the authorities. Valerie has a history of disappearing then turning up again," Ryan replied. "Besides, he has enough on his hands with the accident that happened at the wedding of the mayor's daughter."

"Yeah, we weren't invited to the wedding, but we heard

about it," Sam said. He shook a cigarette from a pack and lit it. He took a deep pull, released the smoke, then shook his head. "Crazy, huh, how she got blown off that cliff and just disappeared. You'd think her body would have been found by now. We all searched."

"Sometimes the sea doesn't give up what it takes," Alex said.

Ryan stood, knowing there was nothing else to ask them, no reason to linger. None of them had displayed any suspicious-looking expressions as they'd looked at the photo of Britta. "Well, I appreciate your time and it was nice meeting you all."

"Sorry we couldn't be of help. You going to be around the area in case we do see your woman?" Claybourne asked.

"I'll be around," Ryan replied. He didn't want to give them any information about where he was staying to lead anyone to Britta, so with a small wave, he left the men and headed farther up the dock.

His cell phone rang and he grabbed it from his pocket and checked the caller ID. It was Michael Kelly. "I did some checking into that drug you asked me about," he said when Ryan answered. "I can't find any information on Stinging Flower. It's not in the database and nobody I've asked has ever heard of it."

Ryan frowned with frustration. He'd been hoping to learn more about the drug that had been injected into Britta. "You'll keep digging?"

"Yeah, but I have a feeling at least for now it's a dead end. You sure you don't need me out there? I could help you turn over stones to try to find out what happened."

"No, I don't want two of us asking questions and bringing unwanted attention to all this. I met the captain of the police department. He seems like a sharp guy. I don't want to get him involved in this because I'm afraid he'll dig deep enough to find out that Valerie King isn't who we say she is. The fewer people who know the truth about her, the better. If I have to go to him later, I will. But at the moment I'm trying to keep this as low-key as possible."

"Okay, it's your call," Michael said. "Is she still not remembering anything?"

"Nothing," Ryan replied. "Who knows if she'll ever remember what happened in Boston. I just wish she could remember where she's been since she arrived here in Raven's Cliff."

"You have any ideas at all?"

Ryan frowned once again. "No, not a clue," he finally replied. "But hopefully that will change over the next couple of days."

After he hung up, Ryan remained standing on the dock, staring out at the storm clouds that drew closer. The approaching darkness in the sky filled him with a sense of apprehension.

He was a man trained in dealing with facts, and there was absolutely no factual basis for what he felt in his soul. And what he felt was that there was an evil here in Raven's Cliff and for four days Britta had somehow been a part of it.

Chapter Four

After Ryan left the cottage, Britta carried the bags of items he'd bought her into the bedroom and began to unpack them. Toothpaste, toothbrush, deodorant and hair products went into the bathroom on a shelf, then she pulled out the clothing he'd bought for her.

By the very items he'd chosen for her, she'd guess that he didn't know her as well as she'd thought. She frowned as she pulled out two pairs of baggy sweatpants, one in blue and one in black. There were matching sweatshirts, as well, and both were two sizes too big.

She couldn't remember a lot of things, but she was sure this wasn't her normal choice of clothing. He'd certainly not opted for making a fashion statement, unless it was a bad one.

As she pulled out a pair of flannel pajamas, she stifled a groan. She was relatively certain she'd never slept in flannel pajamas in her life.

More than anything Ryan had said to her, this indicated that their previous relationship had been strictly business. Still, there had been that moment when she'd awakened in the bed and had stared at him seated next to her and a memory had niggled, teasingly trying to make itself known.

For just a moment she thought she could remember the hot taste of his mouth. For one insane second she thought she had a memory of being in his arms, of his hard, muscled body pressed intimately against hers.

She shook the crazy thought out of her head and hung the clothes in the closet. The strange thing was that while there was a sense of comfortable familiarity about him, she also felt just a touch of disquiet where he was concerned. It wasn't exactly fear, but just the feeling that she needed to be wary.

She had no choice but to trust him for the moment, but if she got a sense that he was a real, physical threat, she'd run. She might not know everything about her past, but she'd do whatever necessary to ensure she had a future.

He'd already indicated to her that there had been one attempt on her life while she'd been in his custody. She wondered if a member of the gang she'd testified against had found her here in Raven's Cliff. Had one of them somehow held her against her will? Injected her with the drug that had stolen her memories?

But why would they do that? She'd already been in court and testified. Her memories of the shoot-out that night at the hotel were documented in court files. What good would it do anyone to try to get rid of her now, so long after the fact? It just didn't make sense.

She hoped Ryan came back with some answers. According to what he'd told her, she'd entered the Witness Protection Program. That meant she'd agreed to leave her old life behind. She'd given up her job, the little apartment she'd called home and all her friends.

She had no relatives. She'd lost both her parents three years ago. Thank God they hadn't been alive to see the mess that her life had become.

What she needed to do was focus on where she went from here. Surely Ryan didn't intend for them to be here in Raven's Cliff for too long, and then she'd be relocated.

The last bag she opened was the one she had brought with her from the clinic. Inside was the white gown she'd been wearing when Ryan had found her, along with the necklace that had been around her neck.

She pulled out the gown and ran a trembling hand over the gauzy material. The bottom was dirty and crusted with sand. She'd hoped by touching it, by looking at it closely, a memory would blossom in her head, but all she got was a vague feeling of fear.

The necklace was made of dozens of chunky pretty shells threaded onto a thin piece of fishing line. Where had it come from? Who had made it? And why had she been wearing it and the gown and wandering in the old lighthouse? She ran her hand across the shells.

Go to the sea.

The words were a faint whisper in her ear and she quickly snatched her hand away from the odd necklace, quieting the strange inner voice.

Unsettled even more than she had been, she shoved the items back into the bag and placed them on the floor of the closet, then left the bedroom.

The first thing she did when she returned to the kitchen was check the refrigerator to see what food was in there. It was fully stocked, as was the freezer. Apparently the FBI had the power not only to change who you were, but also to stock a refrigerator with enough food to last a month.

She pulled out a package of steaks to thaw. She'd cook the evening meal tonight, but if Ryan thought she was going to spend the days here cooking and cleaning for him he had another think coming.

Her mother had been a strong, independent woman, a wonderful role model for Britta. Chores at her house had been equally shared between husband and wife, and Britta's father had never treated her mother like "the little woman" whose only job was to cook and clean for him.

A search of the kitchen cabinets yielded a notebook and a pen. She grabbed herself a cold can of diet soda, then sat down at the table to make a list of what she wanted her new life to be. Someplace in the back of her mind she knew it was a desperate attempt to regain control.

She knew she could never go back to the kind of job she'd once wanted, as manager of an upscale hotel. She'd seen enough movies to know that when you entered the Witness Protection Program you not only gave up friends and family, but also any ties to the kind of job you'd once had. She was a bit surprised that she'd been set up as a housekeeper at the Cliffside Inn.

Maybe in her next life she'd be a waitress or a cashier in a grocery store. The degree she'd obtained in hotel management would probably never be used again.

A rumble of thunder broke the silence and a small sliver of fear tightened her stomach muscles. Funny, she didn't think she'd ever been afraid of storms before, but the kitchen was suddenly too small, too dark, and the approaching storm touched off an unexpected edge of anxiety.

She tried to focus on the paper in front of her but jumped and let out a small squeal as lightning flashed at the window, followed by another growl of thunder. Rain began to pelt down, and she found it impossible to sit any longer.

Surely the rain would bring Ryan back soon. It surprised her how much she didn't want to be alone. As another strobe of lightning flashed, she left the kitchen and went into the living room.

At that moment she heard a key in the front door and Ryan came in, dripping water and cursing beneath his breath. "Does the sun ever shine in this place?" he asked, obviously not expecting an answer.

She hurried into the bathroom, grabbed a towel, then returned to the living room and handed it to him. He flashed her a grateful smile as he swiped it over his short brown hair.

She curled up in one corner of the sofa and fought the impulse to jam her hands over her ears as the thunder crashed overhead. A vision flashed in her head…she saw the hotel lobby decorated in gold and orange for the holiday. The lobby of the Woodlands Hotel offered lush elegance and an aura of luxury and serenity. But that vision was shattered by the acrid scent of gunfire that filled her nose. In her mind she saw one man dive for cover behind a love seat and another topple over the back of a chair. A scream. A moan. And blood. Blood everywhere.

The vision disappeared as quickly as it had come. "Are you all right?" Ryan asked, eyeing her curiously.

"I'm… I think I just had a memory."

He tossed the damp towel to the tile floor and moved to the sofa to sit next to her, bringing with him the odor of the rain and that faint scent that stirred something deep inside her. "A memory of what?"

"The shooting that night at the hotel. It was just a flash. I smelled the gun smoke, saw men diving for cover and that was it. But that's a good sign, isn't it? Maybe with time I am going to get back all of my memories."

He nodded, his gaze enigmatic as it lingered on her. "It's a start," he finally said.

"The days I've been missing since I arrived here, do you think it's the work of one of the gang members?" she asked.

"I don't think so. If one of the gang members had found you, they wouldn't have kept you for four days, but at this point I'm not ruling out anything."

She frowned thoughtfully. "I can understand them wanting to kill me before this all went to trial, but if I already testified against them, then why would they still want to kill me? Why did I have to go into Witness Protection after the trial was over?"

"Several reasons. First of all, we never got the specific shooter who killed our agent. Although you insisted you saw him perfectly, he wasn't among the men we rounded up. Those men you testified against were all tried on a variety of charges, but the man we most wanted escaped. Because you saw that shooter we've always known that there was a possibility of you being our star witness in a new trial. The second reason is revenge, pure and simple. These are real bad guys and reputation is everything. If you testify against them and they let you get away with it, then that diminishes their reputation."

She noticed there was no trace of his lazy Texas drawl at the moment. He stood and plucked at his wet T-shirt. "I'm going to change into some dry clothes. There's no point in me going back out until this rain passes."

He dug around in his suitcase, sitting open in one corner of the room, then pulled out a clean T-shirt and a pair of jeans. "You okay?"

"I guess. I've spent most of the time you've been gone today trying to figure out what happens to me when we leave here."

"We get you relocated someplace else and you build a new life," he replied, making it sound as easy as packing a bag.

"But no matter where I go, these people, these gang members will be looking for me." Even though she tried to suppress it, her fear was rife in her voice.

He dropped his clean clothes on a nearby chair, then once again sat next to her on the sofa. He reached out and took her hand in his. As his long, warm fingers curled around hers, confusion filled her head.

He'd told her their past relationship had been a strictly professional one and yet she was struck with the feeling that this wasn't the first time he'd held her hand.

"I promise when we leave here, I'll get you settled someplace where you'll be safe," he said. "You'll have a new name, a new occupation and we'll get you far away from Boston. This gang isn't everywhere. They're a local gang and their power isn't all reaching." A frown raced across his forehead. "I don't know why they kept you in the New England area to begin with, you should have been sent someplace farther away than here."

She stared down at their hands. She wasn't sure why, but his touch evoked contradicting emotions inside her. On the one hand, it felt comforting and familiar with an edge of excitement. On the other hand, his nearness to her, his fingers entwined with hers, made her feel vaguely threatened.

He jerked his hand away from hers and abruptly stood. "I hope you figured out what's for dinner. I'm used to eating around five o'clock." He grabbed his clothes from the chair and disappeared into the bathroom.

She stared after him, irritation replacing her fear. He had to be right. Their previous relationship had to have been strictly professional, for surely there was no way she'd have any other kind of a relationship with a man who was as irritating, as chauvinistic as Ryan Burton seemed to be.

RYAN STOOD beneath a lukewarm shower, trying to ignore his weakness where Britta was concerned. He'd always considered himself a strong man. He'd had to be strong to survive the childhood he'd been handed. As if surviving the battlefield of his parents' marriage hadn't been enough, years of military training followed by his FBI work should have increased his strength, not just physically but emotionally.

And yet Britta made him weak. She made him forget that he had vowed a long time ago to hold himself detached from any woman who might blow into his life. Short-term affairs were fine, but he had no desire to let anyone in on a permanent basis and he didn't intend to change his mind for one beautiful Norwegian blonde.

The second he'd taken her hand in his he knew he'd made a mistake, but she'd looked so scared, so lost, and all he'd wanted to do was ease some of that fear. But the moment he'd taken her hand in his he'd wanted to go further, he'd wanted to draw her into his arms, feel the warmth of her silky smooth skin against his.

He got out of the shower, dried off, then pulled on a clean pair of jeans and a T-shirt. By the time he left the bathroom he felt better able to cope with Britta.

She was in the kitchen, seated at the table, a notebook and pen in front of her. "What are you doing?" he asked as he rummaged in the cabinets looking for a can of coffee.

"I've been trying to decide where I want my new life to begin when this is all over." She leaned back in the chair and frowned thoughtfully. "What do you think about Seattle?"

"Too rainy," he replied.

"What about Arizona?"

"Too dry."

She grinned at him. "I can see you're going to be no help." Her smile fell and she looked at him curiously. "Why did I come here to Raven's Cliff? I mean, who decided it?"

Ryan found the coffee container and began to make a pot. "It was FBI Agent Michael Kelly who set up this location and the job working at the inn. He came late onto your case. The agent before him was Bill Rankin, who set you up with your new identity."

"All these people, it would be nice if I could just remember one of them."

"You wouldn't remember Kelly, you never met him in person." As the coffee dripped into the glass carafe, Ryan leaned against the cabinet to wait for it to finish. "Kelly told me he picked this village after seeing an ad in a tourist magazine for a housekeeper at an inn. He figured it would be a good fit for you. Coffee?"

She nodded and stared at the paper in front of her where he noticed nothing had been written. He poured them each a cup of coffee, then placed a sugar bowl on the table, knowing she liked her coffee sweetened.

"Doesn't look as if you've made much headway in picking a place to start a new life." He sat in the chair opposite her.

She smiled ruefully. "It's more difficult than I thought, trying to decide on a place to start again. Boston was always my home. I don't know anything else." Her smile faded. "One thing is certain, you have to buy me some different clothes. I appreciate what you got for me, but they're all too big and too hot."

He'd intentionally bought the clothes big, figuring if she looked like a bag lady it would make things easier on him. "It isn't as if you're going to be modeling in a fashion show," he replied. "As long as they are serviceable."

She shook her head, a mutinous expression on her pretty face. "If you have the receipt, you can take back the things I haven't worn. If you don't want to do that, then I'll...I'll just go naked. It's bad enough I feel as if I'm living somebody else's life. I hate the feeling of wearing somebody else's clothes."

Ryan nodded curtly, taking her threat half-seriously and the last thing he needed was a naked Britta in the house. "I'll take care of it tomorrow."

"Thank you." She picked up the pen and made a series of doodles on the paper, then dropped the pen and looked at him once again. "So, you didn't find out anything while you were out."

He took a sip of the coffee, then set the cup down. "I found out that the fishermen in the area are making a killing pulling in record fish. I heard that some stranger has bought an abandoned seaside cottage close to the old lighthouse and that Camille Wells's body still hasn't been found."

"The mayor must be beside himself," she said, remembering the article she'd read in the newspaper the previous morning. "What happened was horrible."

"From what I heard he's back at work, business as usual."

"That seems rather cold," she observed.

Ryan shrugged. "What good is it for him to sit at home? He might as well work while the search teams do their thing."

Britta looked toward the window where the rain still fell in sheets. "There won't be any search teams working today."

"According to the locals, Camille's plunge off the cliff and the lack of spring sunshine is just part of the curse of Raven's Cliff."

"The curse?" She eyed him curiously.

"Yeah, the curse of Captain Earl Raven. Sometime in the late 1700s it seems the good captain was sailing from England to Maine with his family to settle on a sprawling estate he'd bought to start a new life. As they neared the coastline a storm erupted and he lost his wife and two small children at sea. He settled here and built the lighthouse so that no other ships would wreck on the same rocky shoreline that he did."

Ryan paused to take another drink of his coffee, then continued. "Anyway, the legend goes that the Captain had promised that life in Raven's Cliff would be idyllic as long as the lighthouse keeper promised that every year on the anniversary of his wife's and children's deaths, the light would be shone on the rocks where they died. For years Raven's Cliff prospered as each keeper of the light honored the tradition."

"But somebody must have messed up if there's now a curse," Britta said.

He nodded. "A descendant of the captain named Nicholas Sterling III. Five years ago, apparently, he didn't light the rocks that he was supposed to on the anniversary. Nobody knows for sure what happened, but apparently his grandfather tried to light the lamp and a fire ensued. His grandfather was burned to death, and rumor has it that Nicholas wound up jumping from the top of the lighthouse into the sea. That night a category-five hurricane hit, nearly wiping Raven's Cliff off the map. When the storm had passed, Nicholas Sterling was gone, his grandfather was dead and Nicholas's fiancée, Rebecca Johnson, was missing. Two other people died that night and a curse was born."

"Do you believe in curses?" she asked, her eyes as clear and blue as the skies he'd left behind in Texas.

"I'm an FBI agent. I've been trained to believe in facts and evidence. What about you?"

"I'm from Norway, our culture is rich in legends and myths." She released a small sigh. "If there is a curse here in Raven's Cliff, then I feel as if I've become part of it."

Her shoulders slumped slightly and she looked so vulnerable he wanted to pull her into his arms and promise her that everything was going to be all right.

Instead he reared back in his chair and looked pointedly at his watch, then at her. "My rumbling stomach tells me it's about dinnertime, and my watch confirms it. How about you rustle up some grub for us?"

Her eyes narrowed, but not before he saw the flash of anger that lit them. Good, he'd rather have her prickly than soft and appealing.

"Did anyone ever tell you that you're an ass?" she asked.

He laughed. "More times than I can count."

Dinner was tense. It was obvious he'd made her mad, and that was just fine with him. It was easier to keep his distance from her when she was angry with him.

He knew exactly what buttons to push, and, unfortunately, because she had no memory of their previous time together, she had no clue how to push his. He had an unfair advantage that he intended to use to keep safe distance between them.

After dinner they cleaned up the kitchen together, Ryan trying to ignore the brush of their hands as she handed him dishes to dry, the familiar scent of her that drifted in the air.

She kept silent, and after the kitchen was cleaned she went into the bedroom and slammed the door behind her.

Ryan found a sheet and a light blanket in the hall closet and made up his bed on the sofa. He placed his gun within easy reach on the coffee table, then shucked off his jeans and T-shirt and, wearing only a pair of briefs, got under the sheet.

Thunder rolled, rattling the windows as another storm moved overhead. Ryan certainly didn't believe in curses, but Raven's Cliff bothered him in a way no town had ever bothered him before.

On the surface it looked like any other quaint New England fishing village, with antique shops, upscale eateries and turn-of-the-century inns, but beneath it all, there was a simmering energy that felt unhealthy.

He tried to tell himself that it was because his first experience in this place had been watching in horror as a prospective bride plunged off a cliff into the raging sea below.

Or maybe it was because he couldn't come up with an answer to why Britta had been wandering around in a white gown and wearing a seashell necklace at the top of the very lighthouse that had spawned the talk of a curse.

Curse or no curse, what he feared most was that he and Britta were not going to get out of the fog-shrouded, storm laden village without their lives being irrevocably changed.

Chapter Five

Britta paced the small confines of the living room, bored to death as she waited for Ryan to return. He'd left the cottage early with a promise to be home around noon. It was now after two, and besides the boredom a little niggle of fear had worried its way inside her brain.

She'd been reluctant to call him on his cell phone, afraid that he might be in a place where the ring of his phone might put him at risk.

She pulled the curtains aside to peer out the window, then, remembering Ryan's admonition that she should stay away from the windows, allowed the curtain to fall back into place.

Where was he? Where could he be? He'd told her to look for him around noon.

What if something happened to Ryan while he was out? What if one of those nefarious gang members found him and killed him? How would she know if something happened to him? How would she know if he were in danger?

Despite her fear for him, she couldn't help but think of what would happen to her if Ryan never returned to the cottage. What would she do? Where would she go?

She threw herself down on the sofa and instantly was engulfed by the scent of him, that fresh, slightly spicy scent that felt so darned familiar.

Of course it was familiar, she told herself. According to him they had spent months together in close quarters. Business associates forced to live together and nothing more, at least that's what he'd told her.

She got up from the sofa and began to pace once again. It was ridiculous to think that there might have been anything more between them. In the past three days that they'd been together, she'd decided she wasn't even sure she liked him. They bickered over the stupidest things, and there had been more than once when she thought he was intentionally picking fights with her. There was still a part of her that didn't quite trust him, and that worried her.

The sound of a key in the door pushed all other thoughts aside as he walked in, alleviating her worry for his safety. "You're late," she exclaimed. "You should have called."

He looked at her in surprise, then narrowed his gaze and gave her a lazy smile. "Gee, sorry. I'm not used to having a nagging wife to answer to." He closed the door behind him and locked it, then threw a large shopping bag on the sofa.

"I'm not nagging," she protested, his response irritating her to no end. "And you couldn't pay me enough to be your wife. What I'm talking about is common courtesy. You said you'd be home by noon and it's now after two. I was worried. I was afraid some of those gang members found you and killed you." She was appalled by the slight tremor in her voice as these words left her mouth.

He stared at her, the smile on his face immediately disappearing. "I'm sorry. You're right. I didn't think about you being worried. I should have called." He jammed his hands into his pockets, looking so appealing she wanted to walk into his arms.

She wanted him to hold her against that muscled, amazing chest of his and take away the hard lump of coldness that had been inside her since the moment she'd awakened in the clinic.

"What's for lunch?" he asked, completely dispelling the momentary flash of insanity she'd just entertained.

"I don't know. Why don't you go in there and figure it out for yourself, because I had lunch at noon when you said you'd be home." Once again she was in a huff and she knew she was being irrational but she couldn't help it.

"I'm not going to spend day after day a prisoner in this place waiting on you with nothing else to do." She put her hands on her hips and glared at him.

He didn't respond but ambled into the kitchen with that loose-hipped gait that made it nearly impossible not to look at his butt, and a fine-looking butt it was.

She followed him into the kitchen and sat at the table as he pulled cold cuts out of the refrigerator and began to build himself a sandwich. "Want one?" he asked.

"No, thanks. I already ate." She waited while he got chips and poured himself a glass of milk. "I'm sorry. I'm not trying to be a witch." She frowned and tugged at a strand of her hair.

"Forget it," he replied. "You're right, I should have called when I knew I was running late. By the way, I finally stopped at the store and returned those clothes and got you some other things."

"Thank you." She'd been waiting for him to do it for the past three days, but at the moment, clothes were the last thing on her mind.

How could she explain to him the utter helplessness she

felt each time he walked out the door and left her alone? How could she make him understand that she felt as if her life had suddenly been pulled out from under her and she was falling and he was the only thing left to steady her?

Even though it had been seven months since she'd lost her job and the life that she'd known, because of her missing memories it felt as if it were only yesterday. She was grieving all over again.

"So, what did you find out today?" she asked, once he was seated at the table across from her.

"Same as yesterday and the day before that. Nothing that moves us any closer to finding out what happened to you." He bit into a chip, his forehead wrinkled with a frown. "I met Hal Smith who owns the hardware store, seemed like a nice guy. Then I met Stuart Chapman who runs the general store. He's got the names of his wife and kids tattooed up and down his arms. Then there's Marvin Smith, Hal's younger brother and he—"

"Stop," she said, and held up a hand in protest. "You're just going to confuse me with all these names and all these people."

"Okay, the bottom line is either I'm asking the wrong questions or I'm asking the wrong people, but so far everyone I've spoken with tells me they've never seen you before."

"How would they know if they've seen me before or not?" she asked.

He hesitated a beat, then said, "I have a picture of you. I've been flashing it around town."

"A picture? Really? Let me see it." She sat up with interest and dropped the hair she'd been twisting between her fingers.

He scowled. "Why? You know what you look like."

"Please, just let me see the photo."

He pulled it from his shirt pocket and slid it across the table to her. Britta picked it up and stared at it. The photo was of both her and Ryan. They were seated in a booth in some kind of restaurant. She wore a light blue dress and he was in a charcoal-gray business suit and they both were smiling. Her first reaction was that he looked as hot in a suit as he did in jeans.

"That was taken the day the jury came back with a guilty charge on one of the men you testified against," he said.

No wonder they were smiling, she thought. It must have been a celebration meal. But did that explain why they were seated so close to each other? Did it explain the casual way his arm was slung around her shoulders? The way she leaned into him? Their body language made them look like much more than *just* business associates.

She stared at him, her mind grappling to make sense of things. If only she could remember. If only she could figure out why there were times when she felt as if she knew Ryan Burton intimately. There were moments when she believed she knew the taste of his skin in the hollow of his throat, knew the deep groan he made when she ran her hand across his lower abdomen.

Then there were other times when she looked at him and she felt that he was dangerous to her, that if she were smart, she'd run as fast and as far away from him as possible.

But run where? And do what? For the moment she was stuck with Ryan Burton, and that realization filled her with a sense of enormous frustration.

"Picture?" he said, and held out his hand.

She gave it back to him. "We look pretty cozy in that shot."

He stared down at the photo for a moment, then tucked it back into his pocket. "Yeah, we were both excited because we knew it was the end of our time together," he replied. "Chip?" He held out a potato chip.

She shook her head. "So, we didn't really like each other?"

Those green eyes of his didn't quite meet hers. "I told you before, we were friendly and pleasant, but that's it. We tolerated each other."

Britta leaned back in her chair. "Well, in that case, I think you can tolerate spending more time with me than you have in the last three days."

He frowned and paused with a chip halfway to his mouth. "What are you talking about?"

"I've been sitting here and thinking about how much better it would be if I were out there on the streets asking the questions right along with you."

"Absolutely not," he replied in a tone that brooked no argument.

But she wasn't going to let his attitude dissuade her from the decision she'd already made. She leaned forward in her chair. "This is my life, Ryan. Whoever injected me with that drug stole my memories. I might not remember a lot of things about my life, but I know who I am and I know with certainty that the night I arrived here in Raven's Cliff I wouldn't have just gone off with some stranger for a night of fun and experimenting with drugs."

"Yeah, so what's your point?" He pushed his plate away and gazed at her with narrowed eyes.

"My point is that maybe if the person who injected me with that drug sees me around town asking questions, he'll show himself. He'll be afraid that I will remember what he did to me. Maybe if I walk around town, go back to that lighthouse, maybe, just maybe something will finally jog my memory, but it's not going to happen with me spending day after day trapped in this little cottage."

Ryan frowned. "It's a stupid idea. We'd be using you as bait."

"You already told me that you're certain it isn't a gang member who's after me. Nobody knows my real name around here. As far as everyone is concerned I'm Valerie King from Chicago. I came here for a job, and something bad happened and we're trying to figure out what it is. Why is it such a stupid idea?"

He scooted back from the table and carried his plate to the sink. "Because I can't guarantee your safety outside these walls. Because I care... I think it's just a reckless idea."

She leaned back in her chair. "Fine, then if you don't want to be a part of my idea, no problem. I'll just do a little exploring in town on my own," she replied.

He slammed the palm of a hand down on the countertop. "Dammit, Britta, you are the most stubborn, aggravating woman I've ever met. That was the problem the last time we had to spend time together. You don't listen. It's a stupid idea and this discussion is over."

He stalked out of the kitchen, leaving her to stare after him in frustration.

IT WAS A STUPID IDEA, Ryan thought as he paced the small confines of the living room. Britta had grabbed the bag of clothes he'd brought in and disappeared into the bedroom, leaving him alone to brood about his failure to gain any answers.

His cell phone vibrated in his shirt pocket and he pulled it out and answered. "Burton."

"Any change there?" Michael Kelly asked.

"None." Ryan sank down on one corner of the sofa.

"She still doesn't remember anything?"

Ryan sighed. "She doesn't remember and I'm not getting

any answers from anyone I've talked to here in town. What about you? Have you found out anything more about the Stinging Flower drug?"

"Nothing, but I do have some other news you might find interesting. Joey McNabb was found dead last night, murdered in his bed and his right-hand man, Lorenzo Taylor, was gunned down this morning in an alley."

"Wow, that is news," Ryan replied. Joey McNabb had headed the Boston Gentlemen since the gang had first begun.

"We think they were killed by one of their own, that there's an internal battle going on for power. I'd say that's good news for Britta. They'll be far too distracted by their own problems to be thinking about her."

"That is good news. Maybe they'll all kill themselves and we won't have to worry about them anymore." Ryan gripped the phone more tightly against his ear as Britta entered the room.

She'd changed from the oversize baggy sweats to a pair of shorts that displayed her long, shapely legs and a T-shirt that hugged her rounded, firm breasts. He should never have bought those damned shorts. Instantly the living room felt too small and too hot.

"How long are you giving this?" Michael asked. "How long do you plan to stay there?"

"As short a time as possible," Ryan replied as he tore his gaze from Britta, who had sat on the opposite end of the sofa. "But I'm not leaving here without some kind of answers." He frowned and got up and moved to the front window to stare outside where, as usual, gray skies hung low overhead.

"Something isn't right here. My instincts are all screaming that this town is sick—" He broke off, wondering if his fellow FBI agent thought he was the one who was sick—sick in the head.

"Are you sure you don't need me out there? I'm unassigned at the moment, and you know how much I hate being inactive."

"There's nothing for you to do here right now, but I'll let you know if things change." Ryan turned away from the window. "I'll keep you posted and you let me know if you manage to dig anything up on that drug." He clicked off and tucked the phone back into his pocket.

Britta's pale blue eyes studied him intently. "The town is sick? What do you mean by that?"

He sat in the chair across from the sofa, not wanting to be near enough to her that he could smell the clean fragrance of her hair or the familiar scent that was hers alone.

"I'm not sure how to answer," he replied. "It's just a gut feeling that things aren't right in Raven's Cliff." He frowned thoughtfully. "It started on the day of the wedding when I saw a man give the mayor what looked to be a wad of money. The mayor immediately shoved it into his pocket in a furtive way, as if the whole thing was a deep, dark secret."

"You think the mayor is doing something illegal? That he's on the take or something?" She leaned forward, her brow puckering between her pale, perfectly arched eyebrows as she concentrated on what he was saying.

"I don't know." He got up, too restless to remain seated. "Maybe I'm feeling uneasy about this place because of what happened to you or maybe it has something to do with the fact that on the first day I arrived a young bride was blown off a cliff and they still haven't found her."

"She's in the sea." Britta gazed off and a dreamy expression swept over her features. "She went to the sea." Her voice suddenly had a singsong quality, just like it had the night that he'd found her in the lighthouse.

"Britta!" he said sharply, and sat on the sofa next to her.

Her unfocused gaze found his, and the vague expression on her face disappeared as panic took its place. She grabbed hold of his forearm, her fingernails biting into his bare skin. "What just happened?" she asked. "Oh, God, what did I do?"

Ryan eyed her closely. "You zoned out for a minute. Are you okay?"

Without warning, she released her hold on him and instead threw herself into his arms. He stiffened at the sensual assault, the scent of her filling his nose, the warmth of her curves in his arms. He desperately tried not to remember making love to her until they were both gasping and sated.

He wanted to escape her very nearness, and yet at the same time his arms enfolded her as she began to cry. She buried her head in the crook of his neck, her heartbeat palpable beneath the press of her breasts against his chest.

He didn't know exactly what had caused her tears, but her obvious distress broke his heart. Maybe it was because in the months they had shared together he'd rarely seen her cry. But on the rare occasions she had, he'd been a sucker for her tears.

"Shh," he said as he patted her back. "Don't cry," he said gruffly. As irritated as he'd often gotten with her, he'd never liked to see her weep.

"I just feel so lost." Her warm breath against the hollow of his neck felt far too good and reignited memories he wished would stay buried deep in his mind.

What bothered him as much as her tears was the momentary blankness of her features a few moments earlier, the strange fugue state she'd seemed to fall into when she'd mentioned the sea.

"Please, sir, take me back to the sea," she'd said when he'd found her in the lighthouse. Then she'd had the same blank look in her eyes and her voice had held the same strange singsong rhythm.

Maybe it was just the stress of the situation, he thought. He couldn't imagine just waking up one morning and discovering he had lost months of his life. "Britta, it's going to be all right. We're going to figure things out."

She finally raised her face to look at him. "You promise?"

He nodded. "I swear."

Before he recognized her intent, before he could stop it from happening, she rose and placed her lips against his. Instantly heat soared through him, and someplace in the back of his mind he knew he needed to pull away, to stop this before it even began.

But even as he thought this, he made the mistake of kissing her back. The sweetly familiar contours of her lips opened beneath his, allowing him to deepen the kiss to mind-blowing proportions.

His tongue swirled with hers as she molded her body closer to his, so close he could feel the press of her nipples through her thin T-shirt.

Without warning she tore her mouth from his and jumped back out of his arms and off the sofa. She stared at him, then lifted a hand and touched her lower lip.

"I know you," she whispered. "I know the taste of you."

Dammit, he so didn't want to go there. Ryan stood, as well, and faced her, but he wasn't sure what to say.

Her eyes held a hint of accusation. "Tell me the truth, tell me about our relationship before I lost my memories."

He didn't want to talk about it. He didn't even want to think about it, but he knew he had to tell her something. She wouldn't let it rest until she had an answer.

And there was no way in hell that he intended to tell her the truth. "We didn't have a relationship," he said firmly. "There was just one night we both had a little too much to drink and we slept together."

He watched as her eyes widened slightly, then narrowed. "It was no big deal, we both knew it was a huge mistake and that was the end of it," he hurriedly added. "Hell, we spent most of our time together fighting." At least that much was true.

She touched her mouth once again then dropped her hand to her side and straightened her shoulders. He couldn't tell if she believed him or not.

But one thing was certain—if and when she regained all of her memories, she was probably going to hate him more than any man on the face of the earth.

Chapter Six

Britta was up and dressed by dawn the next morning. She'd had a restless night, playing and replaying that kiss in her mind, and analyzing what Ryan had said had taken place between them in the past.

She didn't believe him. Britta didn't remember anything that had happened in the past seven months of her life, but she knew with certainty that she would never drink too much, then fall into bed with a man she wasn't at all sure she even liked, a man who was nothing more than a professional bodyguard. She just wasn't that kind of woman.

She didn't believe him and therefore she was back to the trust issue. She couldn't figure out why he would lie to her, but the result was that she couldn't completely trust him.

She'd awakened that morning with the decision that she didn't care what he had to say about the matter, she was leaving this cottage today and was going to ask some questions of her own.

The faster they solved the missing four days of her life, the sooner she could get away from Ryan Burton and get on with her life, whatever that life might be.

Dressed for the day in a pair of jeans and a bright blue

T-shirt, she left the bathroom and crept into the living room where Ryan lay sleeping on the sofa. The blanket had slipped down to his waist, exposing his firmly muscled, naked chest. Definitely an awesome chest, she thought.

As she stared at him, a vision exploded in her head. Ryan standing in front of a bathroom mirror, a navy blue-and-white-striped towel riding low around his waist and shaving cream smeared on his chiseled lower jaw. She'd wielded the razor, and as their laughter rang in her head the memory faded.

Was it real? It only served to confuse her even more. And if it wasn't real, then was it possible the drug she'd been injected with was producing some sort of false memory?

She went into the kitchen and started the coffee brewing. She'd just poured herself a cup when she heard the sound of the shower running and knew Ryan was up and about.

That kiss they'd shared had rocked her world. It wasn't just because there had been a strange sense of déjà vu about it. It was the fact that her response to him had been immediate and intense.

She'd stopped the kiss, but she'd wanted more. In those few minutes that his mouth had been on hers she'd felt more alive than she had since waking in the clinic. She'd wanted him to strip her clothes off her, she'd wanted to feel his lips lingering over her naked body.

By the time he came into the kitchen she'd downed a cup of coffee and felt mentally prepared to do battle with him. He murmured a good morning, then poured himself a cup of the brew and sat across from her.

"I've been thinking about what you said yesterday," he began.

"I said a lot of things yesterday," she replied. "Which one

have you been thinking about?" She tried not to notice how his white T-shirt pulled across his strong shoulders, how the scent of shaving cream and minty soap wafted from him.

He took a sip of his coffee, his green eyes studying her above the rim of the cup. "The one where you go out with me today and we see if something or someone here in town jogs your memory."

She sat up straighter in her chair with surprise. "I thought I was going to have to fight with you this morning to get you to see things my way," she said.

"I'm still not convinced it's a great idea, but it's obvious that my plan isn't working." Once again he took a sip of his coffee, his gaze going to the nearby window where a glimmer of the sun was peeking through the morning clouds.

Britta kept silent, knowing he wasn't finished and afraid if she said anything, he might change his mind and demand that she stay inside as she had done the past three long days.

She desperately wanted to do something that at least gave her the illusion of control, of being proactive in chasing her elusive memories and getting back some semblance of her life.

Ryan looked back at her once again. "I spoke to my boss late last night and bounced some things off him, trying to figure out the best way to handle this situation. Although I have some reservations, I think maybe it would be best if we speak to Patrick Swanson."

She frowned. "Who is he?"

"The chief of police here in Raven's Cliff. I met him the day of Camille Wells's wedding. He seemed like a stand-up kind of man."

"And do we tell him everything? About me being in the

Witness Protection Program and testifying against those gang members in Boston?"

Ryan shook his head. The sun shining through the windows caught the lean angles of his face and made him appear both devastatingly handsome and more than a little bit dangerous. "No, we only tell him what he needs to know, and that's the fact that you arrived here to begin working at the inn and somebody took you and injected you with drugs. I'll play the role of your FBI boyfriend."

"That will be a stretch," she said wryly, but instantly her head filled with thoughts of the kiss they'd shared.

He ignored her. "I'll tell him I'm working this unofficially but decided to introduce myself as a professional courtesy."

"Whatever you think is best," she replied.

His green eyes were flat and cold. "But the only way I'm agreeing to this is if we do it my way."

"Golly, what a surprise," she said with mock astonishment.

Again he ignored her comment and continued, "My main priority is to keep you safe, so if we're out and I tell you to hit the ground, you hit the ground. If I tell you to jump into the ocean, then that's what you do. No questions, no hesitations. I have to know that you'll obey me for your own safety."

She started to make a joke, but the deadly serious expression on his face stopped her. "I'm not a complete fool, Ryan," she said softly. "I have no desire to get myself hurt or killed, but like you, I want answers. I want to know who drugged me and why."

"Good, then you make sure you do whatever I tell you to and hopefully we'll get those answers." He took another sip of his coffee, a frown furrowing his forehead. "The problem is we don't know where exactly the threat might come from.

We don't know who we're looking for, and that makes keeping you safe a little more complicated."

"But maybe I'll remember something once we get outside and then we'll know exactly who we're looking for and why," she replied. She had to be optimistic. She had to believe that her memory would return, and she couldn't stop the excitement that soared through her at the thought of leaving the cottage.

"Okay, after breakfast we'll head out. Maybe the inn is a good place to start. We can pick up your personal belongings, and perhaps something in that area of town will jog your memory."

It was just after nine when Britta walked out of the cottage and drew a deep breath of the salt-scented air. The feeling of optimism had clung to her through breakfast. Surely today she'd remember something important.

"At least the sun is shining," Ryan said as he opened the passenger door of his car and gestured her inside.

She slid into the seat and watched as he walked around the car to the driver's side. The minute he'd walked out the cottage front door she'd felt the tension that straightened his shoulders and narrowed his gaze.

It was obvious that he was on duty, aware of all the surroundings as he looked first one direction, then the other. At least physically she felt safe with him.

His jeans hugged his long legs, and beneath the dark blue lightweight windbreaker was a navy polo shirt and his gun. It still surprised her, what her life had become, the fact that she needed a bodyguard with a gun.

He got into the car and flashed her a tight smile. "Don't forget I'm in charge."

"You like that, don't you? Being in charge."

He started the engine and grinned at her. "That's the way life is supposed to work—the man is in charge."

"While the little lady works to make his life more comfortable," she added.

He winked at her. "Now you're catching on," he said, his drawl thick as the fog that shrouded the village at night.

"You're a male chauvinist pig."

"Sounds about right," he agreed affably as he backed out of the driveway.

She had a feeling he was playing a role, hiding the real man behind the mask he presented. How well had she known him before? And what would it take to bring down the walls he kept erected around himself?

As he headed toward the Cliffside Inn, she rolled down her window to allow in the fresh air. "I can't tell you how wonderful it is to be out of that cottage," she said. "I've been going stir-crazy. Maybe we can get lunch out?" They'd already passed several restaurants that looked interesting.

"We aren't here on vacation," Ryan said sharply.

"I know that, but eventually we have to eat," she returned evenly. It was as if he was looking to pick a fight every time she opened her mouth.

"We'll see how things go," he said, his voice softer, as if he knew he'd snapped at her.

She focused her attention out the window. Before, when he'd driven her to the cottage from the clinic she'd scarcely noticed the town zipping by. She'd been more concerned about where he was taking her and what happened next.

The sun shining overhead played on colorful awnings stretched over the doorways of quaint gift shops and eateries.

Flowerpots spilled brilliant blossoms of spring flowers in front of establishments, enhancing the aura of a quaint, picturesque village.

How could Ryan think this place was sick, with the sun shining and people meandering down the streets as if there wasn't any other place they'd rather be?

"I think this looks like a lovely place," she finally said, breaking the silence that had descended between them.

"If there's one thing I learned a long time ago it's that most things look nice on the surface, it's only when you scratch a little deeper that you see the ugly."

"And you're sure there's ugly here?"

He frowned, the gesture doing nothing to detract from his handsomeness. "Aside from the fact that something strange happened to you here, I can't explain it. It's just a gut feeling I have."

"Well, don't think about it today," she exclaimed. "The sun is shining and I'm finally out of that boring little cottage and I'm feeling very optimistic about seeing something that will make my memory come back."

She had to believe that all her memories were going to come back today. Then she and Ryan could part ways and she could get on with her life.

"That would be nice. I'm just as eager as you are to get out of this town." Within minutes they had parked and were walking toward the Cliffside Inn.

Britta stared at the beautiful three-story historical home turned inn, hoping for an explosion of memory to fill her head. An old "Victorian lady," the house was set on an acre and a half of perfectly manicured lawn and was within walking distance of the coast and shops and restaurants.

Nothing. She couldn't remember ever seeing this place before this moment. She tried not to be discouraged as Ryan rang the bell next to the front door.

"The innkeeper's name is Hazel Baker," Ryan said as they waited.

A plump woman with faded red hair pulled back in a chignon answered the door. A smile wreathed her face at the sight of Ryan. "Mr. Burton, it's nice to see you again." Her eyes widened as she saw Britta. "Aah, I see you found her. My dear, you had this poor man worried sick." She opened the door wider to allow them inside.

Inside the house was a study in beauty. Hardwood floors gleamed in the sunlight dancing through the windows. Century-old artwork decorated the walls, and the furniture was priceless antiques polished to perfection. A fireplace flanked by two high-backed chairs looked like a perfect place to sip a cup of tea or hot cider.

"I'm afraid I had to go ahead and hire another house-keeper," Hazel said with an apologetic look at Britta. "I'm sorry, Valerie, but I couldn't hold the job for you, not knowing when or even if you'd return."

"I understand, Ms. Baker," Britta replied. It seemed odd to hear herself called Valerie. *But that's who you are now,* she reminded herself. *Valerie King from Chicago.*

"Heavens, call me Hazel, everyone in town does," she replied with a wide smile.

"We've come to get the things she left here," Ryan said.

"Of course. It was just a suitcase. I have it in my office. Please, have a seat and I'll be right back." Her bright yellow caftan whipped around her as she left the room.

When she'd gone, Britta felt Ryan's gaze lingering on her

with an air of expectation. She sighed, fighting a deep wave of depression. "Nothing," she whispered. The optimism she'd felt when she'd left the cottage fizzled away, leaving behind only a deep sense of despair.

RYAN HADN'T REALIZED how much he'd hoped that coming here would solve Britta's amnesia until it didn't happen. Her disappointment couldn't be any greater than his. Each minute he spent in Britta's company was a particular form of torture, and he wanted to get this mystery solved before he did something stupid again.

"Here we are," Hazel said as she carried in a large floral cloth suitcase. She set it on the floor in front of Britta.

"That's it?" Britta asked. "That's all I brought with me when I arrived?"

Ryan could guess what she was thinking, that she'd arrived in a new place to begin a new life with only a single suitcase to her name.

"That's it, dear. That's all you had with you the night you arrived."

"Hazel, I know this might sound like an odd request, but would it be possible for us to see the room where Valerie was going to stay?" Ryan asked.

Although the innkeeper looked puzzled, she shrugged her plump shoulders. "Of course. Nobody has been in there since Valerie arrived, then disappeared." She cast a curious glance at Britta, who was looking around the room as if seeking some clue, some sign that she'd once been here.

Ryan knew from his brief time with Hazel when he'd first arrived in Raven's Cliff that the innkeeper enjoyed a good round of gossip. If he wanted to get the word out that Britta was alive and well and looking for answers, Hazel Baker was just the ticket.

"Actually, Valerie has a bit of a problem," he said, and lowered his voice to a conspiratorial tone.

"Oh?" Hazel's eyes widened once again and she took a step closer to him.

"She has no memory of being here or what happened to her from the time she checked in until the time I found her wandering around days later. There are four days that her whereabouts are unaccounted for, and she can't remember any of it."

"Oh, my." Hazel walked over to Britta and took her hand. "You poor dear, that must be frightening."

Britta nodded. "It is."

"Then you don't remember the nice little chat we had over a cup of raspberry tea when you first arrived? Why, you don't even remember me."

Britta's smile held an apology. "I'm sorry," she said, and shook her head. The sun streaking through the window caught on the flaxen strands of her hair, making it look like pale spun silk.

Ryan frowned as he immediately thought of how that hair felt between his fingertips or splayed across his chest.

"Maybe if I see the room where I was going to stay I'll remember something," Britta said.

"Of course," Hazel replied.

Ryan followed as Hazel led Britta down a hallway. He could use a healthy dose of amnesia himself. He wanted to forget every moment that he'd spent with Britta in his arms, with her warm body against his.

The room Hazel led them to was at the back of the house. It

was a small but attractive room done in shades of rose and pinks. An oak-framed double bed was neatly made up with a ruffled flowered spread. A doorway led to a small adjoining bath.

"The last time I saw you we had a nice cup of tea and visited for a little while, then I brought you in here. You told me good night and I thought you went to bed," Hazel said as Britta walked around the room.

She ran her hand across the top of the polished oak dresser, a small frown tugging her eyebrows closer together over the bridge of her nose.

A small shake of her head let Ryan know the room hadn't jogged her memory. Britta looked at the plump innkeeper. "And you didn't see me leave this room that night?"

"No. But obviously you did. You weren't here the next morning when I came to get you. You were supposed to begin work at seven, and when you didn't show up in the kitchen for your daily assignment, I came here looking for you."

Hazel worried her hands together, as if she didn't quite know what to do. She looked first at Ryan, then at Britta. "I knocked and knocked at the door but there was no answer so I used my master key to come in. Your suitcase was on the floor where you'd set it the night before, and it was obvious the bed hadn't been slept in."

"Thanks for letting us see the room," Ryan replied as Britta drifted to the window and peered outside. Her shoulders stiffened and she whirled around to look at him, her eyes shining bright.

"Thank you," she said to Hazel. "We need to go," she said to Ryan, a thrumming urgency in her voice.

They returned to the entry, where Ryan grabbed her suitcase as Britta headed for the front door. They stepped outside.

"Britta," he yelled as she took off at a run, disappearing around the side of the old mansion.

Ryan cursed, dropped the suitcase and ran after her. He caught up to her in a gazebo that was surrounded by rose gardens.

"Dammit, Britta, what do you think you're doing taking off like that?" he exclaimed.

She turned to face him, her body vibrating with energy. "I was here." The words were barely a whisper, as if she feared the sound of her own voice might shatter the memory working its way through her head.

Ryan said nothing as she whirled around with her back to him. "I was here," she repeated. "I remember seeing the gazebo from my window, and it looked so beautiful. There was some fog around the base that made it look as if it was magical, as if it had sprung from a cloud."

She grasped the wooden railing tightly, her knuckles turning white. "It was getting dark, but the night was warm so I left my room, locked the door and came out here to think, to get myself together for my new life and my new identity."

She looked fragile, her slender body silhouetted against the wood. As he watched she reached up and grasped a strand of her hair and began to twist it around and around her finger.

"I was standing here and I heard a noise." She whirled around to face him, her blue eyes wide with fear, and for a moment he knew she wasn't seeing him, but was looking at a vision in her head.

"It's gone," she said, her voice holding a touch of bitterness. "I almost remembered, but it's gone now."

He jammed his hands into his pockets to keep them from reaching for her. She looked as if she needed the support of his strong arms, but the last thing *he* needed was to have her in his arms.

She straightened her shoulders and the pale blue of her eyes intensified. "I will remember," she said vehemently. She stalked out of the gazebo and headed back toward the car. Ryan pulled his hands out of his pocket and followed closely behind. It had been the combination of her vulnerability coupled with her core of steel that had initially drawn him to her.

He picked up the suitcase he'd dropped and stowed it in the trunk of the car. "Where do we go from here?" she asked.

"The police department." He pointed across the town square to the building that housed not only the police but also city hall. "We'll talk to Patrick Swanson, then find someplace nice to have lunch." It was a concession on his part, and he realized it was an attempt to lift the dark shadows of disappointment that had appeared in her eyes.

They had just crossed the street and reached the sidewalk on the other side when a loud boom split the air. Gunfire. Adrenaline surged inside Ryan, and he threw himself at Britta, tackling her to the ground and covering her body with his own as he pulled his gun.

Chapter Seven

Britta was aware of every point of contact her body had with Ryan's. She'd heard the boom, but hadn't had time to process what it might mean until he was on top of her.

His head was raised, eyes narrowed to dangerous slits as he searched the area. His body was tense against hers as seconds ticked by. "Was that a gunshot?" she finally asked, trying to still the panic that tried to take hold of her.

The whole thing was surreal. One minute they'd been walking along and the next she was on the ground because it was possible somebody had shot at her.

"I'm not sure," he replied. "It sounded like it, but lots of things can sound like a gun firing."

She turned her head and saw a couple walking down the sidewalk on the other side of the street. They appeared unaware of any danger, and she felt Ryan's muscles begin to relax.

"I think it's okay," he finally said. "Maybe it was a car backfiring or a noise from the docks." He looked down at her, his gaze still sharp. "I'm going to get up. You stay on the ground until I tell you it's okay."

She nodded and held her breath as he rose to a crouch, then straightened all the way. He continued to scan the area for another couple of minutes and then held out a hand to help her up.

She grabbed his hand and he pulled her tight against him, as if to shield her from any danger. Nothing happened. "Let's go," he said, but didn't remove his arm from around her shoulder.

As they walked toward the police station building he kept her firmly against his side, although he tucked his gun away. Britta wasn't sure whether it was the fact that there were other people out on the streets or if it was that Ryan's body almost surrounded her, but she felt safe and protected.

Once again she had the feeling of familiarity, as if she'd been in his arms a hundred times before. She loved the way he smelled, and while she knew she should be worried it was possible that just moments before somebody had taken a potshot at them, she felt completely protected walking next to him.

They reached the front of the police station building without incident and Ryan dropped his arm from around her. "Just stand inside the door. I'll be right in," he said.

She did as he asked, stepping into the cool interior of the building and watching out the window as he remained just outside the door.

He stood perfectly still but with an alertness that reminded her of an animal seeking prey. He would take a bullet for her. The thought astounded her. This man had taken on the job of keeping her safe at the potential risk to his own life.

It humbled her, and a new respect for him welled up inside her. He'd told her he'd spent time in the military, so he was a man accustomed to putting his life on the line for others.

He finally stepped inside. "I hope I didn't hurt you. I might have overreacted."

She smiled. "I'd rather you overreact than underreact. I'll gladly take a couple of grass stains on my clothes instead of a bullet to the body."

"I heard that sound and I just went on automatic pilot." His gaze still swept the square, then he took her by the arm. "Let's get inside and officially introduce ourselves to Chief Swanson. Let me do the talking. I intend to give him as little information as possible. I don't want him digging into your background too deeply."

Chief Patrick Swanson was an impressive-looking man. Bald and big-boned, he exuded incredible strength. He ushered them into his office and into seats across from his desk. Behind him on the wall were not only framed awards and letters of commendation but also what appeared to be a family photo of him and his wife and five children.

Ryan introduced Britta as Valerie and showed the chief his official identification, then told him about the missing four days in her life and the fact that she'd been injected with a drug. Patrick frowned as Ryan finished.

"And you don't remember anything that would be helpful?" he asked Britta.

"Not really," she replied.

"I'm conducting my own investigation into this and really just wanted to let you know what was going on for courtesy's sake," Ryan said. "And I'd like to ask you a couple of questions."

"Shoot," Patrick replied.

"Have you had any other incidences of missing women here?"

"None," Patrick replied as he leaned back in his chair. "Oh, of course there's Camille Wells but we know what happened to her." He frowned thoughtfully. "Then there was Rebecca Johnson. She was the daughter of a wealthy New York businessman and was engaged to Nicholas Sterling III. She disappeared five years ago in the midst of the hurricane that struck the area. I can't imagine that her disappearance has anything to do with whatever happened to you. Speculation has always been that she was down by the shore when the storm struck and was swept out to sea."

"Doesn't sound as if that would be tied at all to what happened to Valerie," Ryan replied, and stood. Patrick and Britta got up, as well.

"If you find out anything about this drug, you let me know," the chief said. "Here in Raven's Cliff we have zero tolerance for drugs." He looked at Britta. "Your story is definitely an odd one, Ms. King." He looked at her intently and she wondered if he thought she'd just partied with some people and gotten in over her head.

"Still no sign of Camille Wells's body?" Ryan asked as they walked to the office door.

Swanson frowned. "Nothing. I've decided to call off the search-and-rescue teams. She obviously fell into the sea, and for all we know, the currents could have carried her body miles up the coast. Or she sank and got caught up in driftwood or an old fishing net. And speaking of Camille Wells, it probably would be a good idea if you introduced yourself to Mayor Wells as a professional courtesy. His office is on the second floor in this building."

"We'll do that right now," Ryan replied. They murmured their goodbyes.

"I don't think he believed my amnesia story," Britta said when they left the chief's office. "I think he believes I went out partying and something happened and now I'm pretending to have amnesia so my 'FBI boyfriend' won't get mad at me."

"If that's what he thinks, then there's nothing we can do about it," he replied. "I'd prefer he leave this particular investigation to me, anyway. The fewer people who dig around in your life the better."

As they approached the elevator that would take them upstairs, she grabbed him by the arm. "Ryan, you don't think that, do you? You don't believe that I partied with somebody and things just got out of control?"

Ever since he'd told her that the two of them had gotten drunk and fallen into bed with each other, she'd wondered about what had happened to her in those forgotten seven months.

"Please tell me that somehow in the time after the shooting I didn't become that kind of woman," she said. "Please tell me I don't just fall in bed with any man after a few drinks or take drugs or party with strangers."

His gaze had been so hard, so intense since the moment he'd tackled her to the ground, but now it softened. He reached out a hand and tucked a strand of her hair behind her ear. "You aren't that kind of woman, Britta. You never would have gone off partying with somebody you didn't know. You aren't the kind of woman to party at all."

"Thank you," she said gratefully. The elevator door opened and they rode up to the second floor in silence. When they exited the elevator, a sign on the wall pointed the way to the mayor's office, along with a variety of other city departments.

Mayor Wells's office was down a long hallway, and when Ryan and Britta stepped inside, there was nobody at the receptionist desk.

The door just behind the desk that obviously led to the

mayor's inner office was partially open, and strident male voices drifted out.

Britta started for the door, but Ryan stopped her with a hand on her arm. He put two fingers to his lips to keep her silent.

"Listen, Mayor, I know what's going on around here. I've heard things, I've seen things. I'm not stupid," one deep voice exclaimed.

"I don't care what you think you know," the other man said, his voice filled with obvious but tightly controlled anger. "You just keep your mouth shut, you hear me? You keep your mouth shut or you won't have a job here anymore. Now, get back to work and mind your own business."

Ryan yanked Britta back out into the hallway just as a tall thin man stalked out of the doorway and swept past them without a second glance.

"Stay right here. Don't move from this spot," Ryan instructed her, then he disappeared into the mayor's office.

Nerves jangled inside Britta as she waited for Ryan. She wasn't sure exactly what they'd overheard, but it was apparent there was some kind of trouble in the mayor's office.

Ryan returned a moment later and took her by the arm. "Come on, let's get out of here."

They rode back down to the first floor, and Britta didn't say anything until they got outside, where the sun had disappeared behind a bank of dark clouds.

"What happened?" she asked.

"We'll talk about it over lunch," he said. He paused and looked around the town square. "That place look all right for lunch?" He pointed to a restaurant with a burnt orange awning that read the Rusty Bucket.

"Fine," she agreed.

The Rusty Bucket offered a variety of fare but the specialty was seafood. Britta ordered lobster stew and Ryan chose fish and chips. It wasn't until the waitress served their food and left their table that he seemed to relax.

"There's definitely something fishy going on in this town," he said as he stabbed a portion of fish with his fork. "And no pun intended. When I went back to the office I overheard the good mayor making a phone call. Whoever he called, he told the person on the other end of the line that if they weren't careful, all hell was going to break loose. That, coupled with the conversation we overhead, tells me something isn't right."

Britta frowned. "You think he's on the take? You said that at the wedding ceremony you saw somebody hand him a bundle of cash."

"Right now it's just all speculation, but all my instincts are definitely shouting that Mayor Wells isn't on the up and up."

"So, what are you going to do about it?" she asked.

"I'll pass the information on to the appropriate people, but right now I'm not interested in what's going on in local government here in Raven's Cliff. I just want to solve the mystery of you."

She smiled. "I'd say that you're far more a mystery to me than I am to you. You probably know everything there is to know about me, but I don't know anything about you, Ryan."

"You know what you need to know. My job is to protect you, that's all that's important." His eyes were shuttered, as if to keep her from seeing inside him and noting anything personal.

"That's not fair," she replied. "Surely I knew more about you than that when we were together before."

He sat with his back to the wall so he was able to see everyone who walked into the establishment. His gaze swept over her shoulder to the door, then back to her.

"I'm originally from Texas, although my home is wherever my work takes me. I already told you that I joined the Army when I was eighteen and served time before deciding that the FBI was where I wanted to be. I've been working gang-related crimes for the past three years."

She didn't want to know about his work. She wanted to know about Ryan Burton the man. "Where are your parents?"

"Last I heard they were in Texas. We weren't what you'd call a close family." There was a hint of tension in his voice.

"Are you an only child?"

"Yes," he answered curtly.

"And you've never married?"

"Marriage doesn't interest me. Long-term relationships don't interest me." His eyes took on that lazy gleam she'd begun to recognize. "You know us Texas men, we like our steaks rare and our women plentiful."

She leaned back in her chair. "You do that on purpose, don't you?"

"What?"

"Every time the talk gets a little too personal or uncomfortable for you, you turn on that country-boy act to distance me," she said.

He scowled. "That's ridiculous. That's not an act, darlin', that's just who I am. Now, eat up, we've got more work to do this afternoon."

Britta focused on her meal, but her thoughts raced. She wasn't sure why, but she was relatively certain that Ryan was lying to her. That wasn't who he was, and that made her wonder just who the man was who was supposed to have her back in all this mess.

THE THUNDER AWOKE RYAN from the dream. No, not a dream, rather a familiar nightmare. His heart thudded with the scenes from his childhood, visions that filled his mouth with a bitter taste.

He sat up, knowing that sleep would be impossible until the last vestiges of his past left his head. With the benefit of a lightning flash he reached for his jeans at the foot of the sofa and pulled them on, then raked a hand through his hair as if he could pull the memories right out of his head.

It was always the same. The nightmare began with the sounds of voices arguing, angry words spat back and forth between his mother and his father. Soon the angry words became broken dishes and slammed doors and then slaps and punches and screams.

Sometimes Ryan felt as if he'd spent the first ten years of his life hiding in the floor of his closet, praying for them to stop before it went too far, but he'd never had the power to halt the progression of violence.

He got up from the sofa and moved to the window, where he stared out at the falling rain. It had been a long time since he'd had the nightmare, and he suspected that this last one had been prompted by Britta's questions over lunch about his parents.

He and Britta had spent the afternoon pounding the pavement around the square. They'd stopped in at the Tidal Treasures trinket shop where they'd met Lucy Tucker, the bubbly owner, who had spent time sharing some harmless local gossip.

After that they had visited several other shops, but in no place they went did anyone give an indication that they had seen Britta before or that her appearance was particularly surprising.

What he'd been trying to chase down was the origin of the gown and necklace she'd been wearing on the night he'd found her. The necklace and the gown were the only pieces of hard evidence they had. The gown had been hand stitched, and for much of the day they'd gone from shop to shop trying to find someplace that sold that particular material.

They'd also checked out the stores that sold jewelry, looking for a piece that resembled the one Britta had worn around her neck the night he'd found her, but so far no success.

He left the window and went into the kitchen where he turned on the small light over the stove and grabbed a bottle of water from the refrigerator. He twisted the top and took a deep swallow and thought about that morning he'd heard what he'd thought was a gunshot.

His heart had nearly stopped as he'd thrown himself at Britta. He'd spent months of his life keeping her safe and the thought of losing her in this damned village, the thought of losing her at all filled him with an agonizing pain.

He didn't want her in his life, but he wanted her alive and well and eventually happy in a new life where there were no threats against her for her to worry about.

What had happened to her during her missing four days? Who had injected her with the drug that had stolen her memory of those days? And why? The questions nagged at him every minute of every day.

He was ninety-nine percent sure that whatever had happened to her had nothing to do with the Boston Gentlemen.

This wasn't about her past, rather, he had the gut feeling it had something to do about this little fishing village.

Another flash of lightning ripped the night skies, and suddenly Britta appeared in the kitchen doorway. Instantly his body tensed as he tried to ignore how achingly beautiful she looked with her hair sleep-tousled and the skimpy pale blue silk nightgown barely covering her.

"The storm…the thunder woke me, and I remembered something," she said, her voice trembling with emotion. "I remembered somebody coming out of the fog at the gazebo at the inn. It was a man, but I can't remember what he looked like or what he said to me. Oh, and I remembered that you love pepperoni pizza."

He hoped she didn't remember the last time they'd eaten pepperoni pizza. It had been in bed, after a rousing bout of lovemaking.

"I'm right, aren't I?" She took several steps into the kitchen, the dim lighting doing nothing to hide the gleam of her smooth skin.

"Sure, I like pizza," he agreed. What he wanted to do was yell at her to go put some more clothes on, yell at her to take off that damned nightgown and let him make love to her right here, right now. But that would be a monumental mistake.

"Did the storm wake you, too?" She opened the door to the refrigerator and grabbed a can of diet soda.

"Yeah." He sat at the table, wishing she'd take her soda and go back to bed. Instead she joined him at the table.

"I hate storms," she said, and tilted her head back to take a sip from the can.

The slender column of her neck invited his mouth to explore. "Yeah, well, you've obviously come to the wrong place," he said, and tore his gaze from her and looked toward the window. "That's all it seems to do in this place, one storm after another."

"Maybe it's just part of the curse," she replied. "You know, Captain Earl Raven stirring up storms and working a fog machine just to keep everyone on edge."

He was on edge, all right. The real curse was that he couldn't forget the taste of her mouth, the weight of her breasts in his hands. He couldn't get out of his head the feel of her legs wrapped around him as he made love to her, or the tiny mewling sound she made in the back of her throat when he kissed her behind her ear, caressed the smooth skin of her inner thigh.

He took another sip of his water, the liquid wetting his suddenly parched mouth. "I told you before, I don't believe in curses."

"I didn't really, but I'm beginning to feel as if somebody put a curse on my life. I lost my whole life, not just to the amnesia, but to circumstances I couldn't control."

"Nobody put a curse on you. The night of the shoot-out in the hotel in Boston you were just at the wrong place at the wrong time."

"And I was in the wrong place at the wrong time when I decided to go outside and walk to the gazebo outside of the inn."

He couldn't stand it anymore. He had to get away from her. The dimly lit kitchen in the middle of the night was too intimate a setting and she was unaware of her own provocative desirability.

"Are you about done?" He gestured to her can of soda. "I need to get some sleep and I can't do that with you up and wandering the place." His voice was more brusque than he'd intended.

Even the faint light in the room couldn't hide the hurt that swept over her features. "Sorry, I didn't realize I was keeping you up." She took another sip of her soda, then carried the can to the sink, dumped the rest of the contents and threw it away.

Ryan tightened his grip on the water bottle. Distance, that's what he needed. He breathed a sigh of relief as she murmured a good-night and left the room.

Unfortunately, distance was impossible over the next two days. Rain fell in buckets, keeping Britta and him inside the small cottage. They spent much of the first day playing cards at the kitchen table as the rain beat against the windows.

During the months they'd been together before, they'd often played cards to pass the time. This time she beat him more games than not because he was distracted by the scent of her, by the very sight of her in a pair of tight jeans and a lightweight pullover sweater that emphasized the thrust of her breasts.

He'd finally accused her of cheating, which had made her mad and sent her to her room. Which was fine with him. The less he saw of her, the better.

He now stood at the window cursing the weather that kept him trapped inside with her. She sat on the sofa behind him, her very presence creating a knot of tension in the pit of his stomach.

There was an explosion coming. He could feel it, the build-up of pressure inside him, the raw aching need to possess her one more time. It had begun the moment he'd seen her in the clinic, and each minute he'd spent with her since then had only increased his desire.

He should have had this case assigned to somebody else, somebody who had no personal feelings for her. But when he'd heard that she was missing, knew that she might be in trouble, he didn't trust anyone else to do the job as well as he would.

"This damned weather," he finally said, and turned away from the window with a scowl.

Britta looked up from the paperback book she'd been reading. She'd been unusually quiet this morning. Since she'd gotten back her suitcase, she was in clothes she'd obviously picked because they looked good on her. Today she was clad in a pair of jeans and a pink blouse that complemented her blond coloring.

"Are you sure you don't remember anything that you haven't already told me?" he asked as he sat on the sofa next to her.

"You mean, about the four days?"

"What else would I mean?" he asked irritably.

"I thought maybe you might want to know what I remember about the time we spent together in Boston."

His heart lurched uncomfortably and he eyed her uneasily. "You remember things about that time that you haven't told me about?"

"Not necessarily remember, but there are some things I just seem to know."

"Like what?" he asked, his pulse accelerating. Surely she didn't remember everything that had happened between them, because if she had, she wouldn't be looking at him now without rancor, without pain radiating from her eyes.

"I know that you lied to me about our past relationship," she said.

"I don't know what you're talking about," he replied.

"We didn't just have a single night of lovemaking. There was more, much more." Her gaze held his intently. "I remember watching you shave."

He wanted to look away. He wanted to tell her she was crazy, that whatever memories were making their way to the surface weren't real. But instead he gave a curt nod of his head. "Okay, we were lovers for a couple of months," he conceded.

"Thank you," she whispered. "I was afraid I was losing my mind, because I keep getting flashes of you and me together. So why did we stop being lovers?"

"Because we weren't in love," he said flatly. "We both knew the score. I'm thirty-six years old, Britta, eleven years older than you. We were thrown together in an unnatural setting and what we had wasn't real. It was just sex."

"In the bits and pieces I see in my head it doesn't feel like just sex," she replied.

He jumped up from the sofa, wishing the cottage had a hundred rooms so he could get some healthy distance from her. "Just leave it alone, Britta. There are some memories not worth remembering."

He went into the kitchen and hoped she'd take his advice and try not to remember how things had ended between them. He moved to the window and stared out, wondering if there really was a curse, not just on this place but on him, as well.

Chapter Eight

The rain didn't bother him as he drove away from Raven's Cliff. The rhythmic swish of the wipers only served to increase his excitement.

The man couldn't believe his luck. The day before, if he hadn't stopped in that restaurant in the little fishing village forty miles from Raven's Cliff, he would have never known.

As he was eating the special of the day he'd overheard two fishermen talking about the woman that had been pulled from the ocean earlier that morning. A Jane Doe, they'd said. She was badly beaten by the sea and suffering amnesia.

He'd finished the meat loaf and mashed potatoes, his mind whirling with possibilities. Could it be? Was it even possible? His entire body had thrummed with energy as he considered what it all might mean.

He'd left the diner and gone directly to the little hospital located in the tiny village of Ocean Heights. The hospital was hardly more than a clinic, ill-equipped to handle anyone seriously ill. That was fine with him, he'd known it would only work to his advantage if what he suspected was true.

A nurse had taken him in to see their Jane Doe, who had been heavily medicated and sleeping. He'd immediately known who she was and he'd begun the charade that would give him what he wanted most.

Anticipation surged inside him now as he pulled into the hospital parking lot. Initially he hadn't been sure he could pull it off, but the staff was obviously eager to release Jane Doe into the custody of somebody who would see her transferred to a facility where she could get better care.

He parked, patted his breast pocket where he had all the falsified documentation he would need, then grabbed his umbrella and got out of the car.

The rain pattered down, but how could he mind a little rain when he was on the verge of a stroke of luck that would assure him success?

Inside the hospital the scent of antiseptic and alcohol hung in the air. His feet made barely a sound as he headed toward room 112. "Jane Doe" was in a wheelchair, her head slumped forward as she slept. Her bruised and swollen face was almost unrecognizable. Almost, but not quite.

"There you are," the nurse greeted him with a bright smile. "We have her all ready to go with you." She tucked a blanket more closely around the sleeping woman. "We have her fairly well medicated for the trip. She should be comfortable."

"I can't tell you how grateful I am for the care you've given my daughter," he said. "She's my only child, my precious little girl. You know we were sailing and having such a great time and the storm blew up and…" He allowed his voice to crack. "One minute she was on deck and the next minute she was gone. I thought I'd lost her forever."

"She's going to need some special care," the nurse said, keeping her voice low.

"The best," he replied. "She's going to get the best care that money can buy. I've already arranged for her to go to a private clinic where all her needs can be met until she can come back home to me."

"Let me get the paperwork you need to sign and we'll let you both be on your way. I'll be right back." She smiled, then whirled out of the room, leaving him alone with the woman in the wheelchair.

It was amazing that she was alive. She'd obviously taken a beating against rocks and driftwood and who knew what else. If her face hadn't been so swollen and discolored it was possible somebody else might have recognized her and what he was about to do would have been impossible.

But within minutes it would be done and she'd be his. He tamped down his excitement, knowing it wouldn't do to look too eager to get her out of here.

The nurse returned with the paperwork and went over the doctor's instructions with him, then he signed the appropriate forms and showed her the false identification he'd prepared.

Within minutes the nurse was wheeling her out into the night where the rain had stopped. It was as if providence was smiling on him as he helped the nurse transfer the patient from the wheelchair into the passenger seat of his car.

She stirred, her eyes opening to stare at him dully as he fastened the seat belt around her. "There you are, my dear," he said gently for the benefit of the watching nurse.

Once she was settled and safely buckled in, he said his goodbye to the nurse and got into the car with his precious passenger.

"Don't worry, I'm going to take very good care of you," he said as they pulled out of the hospital parking lot. He thought of the place he'd already prepared for her, a place where nobody would find her.

The underground cave beneath the old Beacon Manor lighthouse was the perfect place to keep a treasure, and she was his treasure, at least for now.

He glanced over at her and smiled. "Why don't you try to take a little nap. We have a bit of a drive ahead of us."

She nodded and with a small sigh Camille Wells leaned her head back and closed her eyes.

Chapter Nine

Britta and Ryan walked across the town square to the diner for breakfast. Although the clouds were low and heavy looking, no rain had fallen, and they'd finally been able to get out of the cottage.

The night before had been tense and strained after their conversation about their past relationship. Of course, it really hadn't been a conversation, Britta thought as they entered the diner and he gestured her toward a table in the back of the busy place.

Ryan slid into the chair facing the door and Britta sat opposite him, noting how the young women at the next table eyed him appreciatively.

And why wouldn't they? Ryan's buff physique was displayed to perfection by his tight jeans and clinging white T-shirt. The short buzz-cut hair emphasized the chiseled lines and angles of his handsome face. He nodded to them with an affable smile.

The morning had been as tense as the night before. She'd been grateful when he'd suggested breakfast out, anything to alleviate the pulsating energy between them was fine with her.

Somehow she hadn't been surprised to learn they'd been lovers. What did surprise her was the desire for him that resonated deep inside her. She was acutely aware of him every minute of every day.

Little things that he did stirred the faint whisper of memory from another time. The way he tugged at his chin when in deep thought, the crinkle at the corners of his eyes when he gave her that devilish grin. She wanted him and she wasn't sure what to do about it.

She now picked up a menu and studied it, consciously shoving thoughts of Ryan and lovemaking away. As she scanned the menu, she absently listened to the lively conversation going on among the women at the table next to them.

"Nobody has seen him since he moved in a couple of weeks ago," one of the women said. "Jenny at the grocery store said they deliver his groceries and leave them on the front porch and he leaves cash in an envelope there to pay for them."

"That's so creepy," a young busty blonde replied. "I heard he's a millionaire and that his name is Ingram Jackson. If he's so rich I can't imagine why he's living in that old run-down cottage."

"I thought the town was supposed to demolish all those old places by the fish-packing plant," the third woman, a pretty brunette, at the table said.

"At the moment I think the mayor has other things on his mind," the blonde said, and for the next few minutes the conversation revolved around the tragedy of Camille Wells and her fall from the bluffs.

It was the blonde who took the topic back to the man who had apparently recently moved into town. "Don't you think it's weird that nobody has seen him since he moved here?" she asked. "Don't you think he'd have to leave the house for something? A new shirt or a pair of shoes."

The brunette laughed. "Not everyone is a shopaholic like you are, Heather."

"I heard he only goes out at night like some vampire or something," Heather replied.

"Too weird," one of them said.

As their conversation turned to a new dress shop that had opened its doors in town, Britta set her menu aside and looked at Ryan, who had apparently been eavesdropping on the conversation, as well.

"Maybe we should check out this recluse later," he said in a low voice. "If what they said is true, he showed up here just before the time you disappeared."

A chill washed over Britta at the thought of some creepy man holding her captive for four days and four nights. For what purpose? She hadn't been sexually abused, thank goodness, and she hadn't been physically harmed except for the drug that had been injected.

Ingram Jackson. She twisted the unusual name around and around in her head, but no emotion was associated with it. Maybe he hadn't told her his name. Maybe he'd just been a scary stranger who had taken her captive for whatever purpose.

"While we're looking for this mystery man, maybe we'll check around the docks and see what we can stir up," Ryan said.

The waitress arrived at their table, and they both ordered waffles and bacon. When she'd left the table, Britta cupped her fingers around her coffee mug and looked at Ryan curiously.

There was no question that their conversation from the night before had played in her head as she'd gone to sleep. His admission that they'd been lovers had filled her with an odd sense of relief.

At least she knew she wasn't going crazy. From the moment she'd seen him sitting in the clinic room she'd had the feeling she'd known him before, that she'd been close to him.

What she didn't understand was his explanation that they'd been lovers but not in love. Although Britta was hardly a prude, she couldn't imagine herself being a man's lover without some kind of love being involved.

She'd only had one other relationship that she remembered, and that had been while she'd been in college. His name had been Jim and they'd been friends for six months and lovers for two. He'd been a nice guy but Britta had realized quickly he wasn't the man of her dreams.

The women at the table next to them finished their meals and left, taking with them much of the cheerful noise in the place.

Britta would have liked to ask Ryan more about their past relationship but she was tired of the tension between them and so didn't want to ask him any more questions, at least for now. She just wanted them to enjoy their breakfast out.

"What are your plans when you're finished here?" she asked.

He shrugged, the gesture tightening his shirt over his broad shoulders. "I go wherever the Bureau sends me."

"Where's home base?"

"A small apartment in Boston. But I'm rarely there. It's mostly just a place to shower and change clothes." He took a sip of his coffee. "Have you thought about where you'd like to be relocated when this is all over?"

"As far away from Boston as possible," she replied quickly. "I don't ever want to worry about crazy gang members finding me again."

"According to my source there's some infighting going on in the gang. Joey McNabb, the head of the Boston Gentlemen, was murdered and his right-hand man was gunned down in an alley. There's apparently an internal fight for control going on."

"That can't hurt my situation, right?"

He smiled, the first genuine smile she'd seen from him in a while. The warmth of that attractive gesture filled her with heat. "That can't hurt. We always love it when these gangs start to fight and fall apart from the inside out. Makes our work so much easier."

"Still, your work is so dangerous. Are you ever afraid?"

He smiled again and took a sip of his coffee before answering. "Only fools aren't afraid, and I'm no fool. Fear is good, it keeps you on your toes."

The conversation halted as the waitress returned with their orders. As they ate, Britta found herself chattering about the parts of her life she remembered, her work at the hotel, her life with her parents and her devastation when they had died in a car accident.

"We lived a simple life when I was young, but once a month my father would take us to a different hotel to spend the weekend. We'd eat in the hotel and I'd swim in the pool and that's when I fell in love with the hotel industry and knew when I grew up I wanted to work in one. Forgive me if you've heard all this before," she finally said. "Needless to say I can't remember what I've told you before and what I haven't."

"Don't apologize. I like the sound of your voice. That accent of yours is charming."

She looked at him in surprise and then laughed. "And I find that Texas drawl of yours totally infuriating because it usually means you're about to say something ridiculously chauvinistic." She chewed a bit of her waffle and eyed him thoughtfully. "And I don't think that's who you are in the heart," she added.

He leaned back in his chair. "Why, darlin', what makes you think I even have a heart," he retorted with a dark glitter in his eyes.

She gave him a lazy smile in return. "It's obvious my memory doesn't serve me anymore, but somehow I think my heart knows yours, Ryan Burton."

His smile fell away. "You're talking nonsense," he replied in a curt tone, and as usual she saw the shutters that closed down over his eyes. "You ready to go?" he asked.

She wasn't ready to leave. For just a few minutes as she and Ryan had eaten their breakfast and made pleasant small talk she'd forgotten she had amnesia, she'd forgotten that the only reason he was here with her was because he was her bodyguard. For a little while she'd forgotten that she was nothing more to him than his latest assignment. They had been just a man and a woman sharing a breakfast together.

They were at the register to pay when a familiar man came in. "Dr. Jamison," Britta said to the man who had taken care of her in the clinic.

The doctor flashed her a tired smile. "Hello, Valerie. How are you doing? Have you gotten over your amnesia?"

"Not completely, but I'm getting flashes of memories here and there. And how are you?"

"Utterly exhausted. I think I've seen more patients in the clinic in the past couple of days than I have in the last six months. There's something nasty going around, but I can't get a handle on it."

"Nasty how?" Ryan asked as he stuffed his wallet back into his pocket.

"Mostly dangerously high fevers and unusual rashes. These cases are definitely putting stress on our little clinic. We need more help than we have."

"I'm sorry to hear that," Britta replied. "Well, good luck," she said as the doctor turned to the waitress to place his order.

"How are we going to find this mystery man," she asked as they left the diner, her thoughts quickly shifting from mysterious fevers to their goal for the day, Ingram Jackson, the peculiar recluse. "Those women at the table next to ours didn't mention a specific address."

"No, but they did mention an old fish-packing plant."

She smiled ruefully. "I would imagine there are several of those in the area."

"If there's one person who would know something about this guy, it would be Hazel at the inn. She seems to know everyone and everything about this town."

As they walked across the square toward the inn, Ryan kept an arm wrapped firmly around her. She wanted to snuggle into his warmth, but she knew the only reason he was doing it was for safety purposes.

As usual Hazel greeted them with friendly warmth and insisted they come inside and share a cup of tea with her. "Tourist season hasn't really officially begun, so things are quiet. This crazy weather isn't helping any," she said as she bustled around to fix the tea. "Raspberry tea always sits well with me."

Once it was ready and they were all seated in the parlor with dainty china cups of the fragrant brew, Ryan asked her what she knew about Ingram Jackson.

Hazel's brow tugged into a frown. "Unfortunately, I can't tell you much about the mystery man. Nobody seems to know anything about him and he certainly hasn't shown himself to anyone in town. I've heard a rumor that he was from the Midwest, then another one that he was from Europe. Who knows what the truth is."

"You know exactly where he's living?"

She nodded and her frown deepened. "Every town has the right side of the tracks and the wrong side, and from what I've heard this Ingram Jackson bought the old Jennings place and that's definitely on the wrong side of the tracks. It's a seedy area, mostly abandoned buildings. That part of town took a hard hit from the hurricane we had five years ago. The town was supposed to tear most of them down, but it hasn't been done yet."

"Do you have a description of the particular cottage this guy has moved into?" Ryan asked.

"It used to be a cheerful yellow, but it's faded now and it's almost directly across the street from the old fish-packing plant. Sits off by itself some. You can't miss it." She eyed the two of them worriedly. "You be careful down there. There's lots of criminal activity around those parts."

At that moment a tall, well-built man walked in. His hair was jet-black and his smoky, gray eyes narrowed slightly at the sight of them.

"Sorry, I didn't mean to interrupt anything," he said.

"No problem, we were just getting ready to leave," Ryan replied.

"Have you all met?" Hazel asked as all three of them stood. "This is Grant Bridges, our assistant district attorney. And, Grant, this is Ryan Burton and his lady friend, Valerie. They're visiting here in town for a while."

Ryan and Grant shook hands, and he nodded and smiled at Britta. "Nice to meet you both," he said. "I was just on my way up to my room."

"Is there anything you need, dear?" Hazel asked.

"No thanks, Hazel, I'm fine." He excused himself and went up the stairs that led to the guest rooms.

"Poor man," Hazel said when he was gone. "He's been lost since the tragedy." Britta looked at her quizzically. "You probably don't know about it," Hazel said in explanation. "He was to marry Camille Wells."

"Oh, I read about what happened to her in the paper," Britta said.

Hazel nodded. "Terrible thing. Grant moved in here before the wedding. The mayor had bought him and Camille a lovely house to move into after the wedding, but now that the wedding didn't take place, who knows what's going to happen."

She walked with them to the front door. "Thank you for the tea, Hazel," Britta said.

"And the information," Ryan added.

She wagged a plump finger at them. "You remember what I said. That part of town isn't a good place to be."

With her warning ringing in their ears, they left and returned to Ryan's car. "When I read that newspaper article about Camille Wells falling off the cliffs, I didn't even think about the man she was supposed to have married that day," Britta said.

"I had been helping with the search effort for Camille when I spied you in the lighthouse. I'd gone to the wedding to mingle with the crowd, see if I could hear anything that might lead me to you. It wasn't just a bad scene, it was…" He paused a moment as if searching for the right word. "It was just bizarre."

Britta tried to imagine the scene in her head, but found it far too horrifying.

"That wind that came up seemed to come from the very

bowels of hell." He tightened his grip on the steering wheel and shook his head. "It had been windy, but that particular gust was something else."

It didn't take very long to reach a part of town that held none of the charm of a New England fishing village.

The cottages were closer together, most still sporting evidence of the killer storm that had hit years before. Many of the cottages were boarded up. Graffiti was spray painted everywhere. Some of the structures listed precariously to one side, the windows broken and never replaced.

On the opposite side of the street was an industrial area, a fish-packing plant no longer in use, several boat shops, a tattoo parlor and liquor store that were open for business.

Without the aid of sunshine, the area looked particularly dismal, although Britta didn't think any burst of sunlight would do much to cheer the place.

Hazel hadn't known the exact address, but as Ryan drove slowly down the street, they looked for a place that fit the description she had given them.

"It's weird not to see any people," Britta said. "The sidewalks in town are always bustling, but here it's like a ghost town." A chill swept through her, one that had nothing to do with the cool outside temperature.

"It is a little creepy," Ryan agreed. "Although I imagine there are people here, they just aren't showing themselves. This is probably an area where drug dealers ply their trade. I'll bet most of the people in this part of town only come out at night like cockroaches."

"There." Britta pointed up ahead where a weathered yellow cottage stood off by itself. A car was parked alongside, but other than that there was no sign of occupancy.

Ryan parked his car but remained behind the wheel, gazing at the house with sharp intensity. He finally turned and looked at her. "Anything jog a memory?"

She stared out the window, seeking any elusive whisper of familiarity, but there was nothing. "No, I feel as if I've never been here before, but who knows if I have." She tamped down an edge of frustration.

Ryan opened his car door. "Let's go check it out. Maybe when you get closer something will connect with you."

Together they walked toward the house. Behind it the sea bubbled and rolled to a shoreline littered with driftwood and trash. The wind had picked up and buffeted them as they walked across the sandy ground.

As they drew closer she could see that all the windows were covered with dark plastic on the inside. It was dark enough to not only keep people from peering in, but also keep the sunshine from lighting any of the interior rooms. Weird, just plain weird.

"Maybe he really is a vampire," she said half-jokingly, but a nervous tension coiled in her stomach, making it cramp uncomfortably.

Ryan pulled his gun from his ankle holster, reminding Britta that danger could come to them from any direction at any time.

The tension in her stomach knotted tighter as they walked up the rickety porch stairs, each one creaking ominously beneath their weight. With Britta squarely behind him Ryan knocked on the door.

"Hello?" he called.

There was no answer. He knocked harder. "Mr. Jackson, we'd like to have a talk with you," he shouted.

Still no reply.

"He's in there, I know he is," Ryan said with frustration. "Come on, let's take a walk around back and see if we can get his attention."

The back of the house looked worse than the front. Here it was impossible to tell that the house had once been yellow as it had weathered to a dull gray. A back porch had once been covered, but the roof was now missing and the remaining posts leaned to one side.

The windows back here were also covered with the dark film that allowed no peek inside. As Ryan approached the door, Britta turned to look at the ocean.

Today it looked as gray and ominous as the clouds that hung low overhead. The waves rolled in, sporting a white crest whipped by the wind.

To the sea.

Go to the sea.

The voice whispered inside her head. Compelling her, demanding her immediate response. Everything around her faded to nothingness as the voice whispered once again.

Go to the sea.

Chapter Ten

Ryan knocked one last time on the door, then stepped back in frustration. He believed Ingram Jackson, or whatever his name was, was inside, but he had a feeling nothing was going to compel him to open the door to a couple of strangers.

The man obviously didn't want to be seen, and although that made him a person of interest in Ryan's mind, there wasn't much he could do about it at the moment.

"He's not going to answer," he said, and turned around, surprised not to find Britta standing right behind him. He saw her in the distance, walking slowly across the beach.

"Britta?" he called to her, but she didn't seem to hear him. He frowned as he watched her. She wasn't walking with her usual sensual grace, but rather like the marionette of a demented puppeteer. Her jerky, uncharacteristic gait filled him with sudden alarm.

"Britta," he yelled again as he jumped off the porch and hurried after her. She was nearly to the water's edge and didn't appear to be slowing down. What in the hell was she doing?

He raced across the sand, horror surging inside him as she reached the water but didn't stop walking. She was knee deep in the surf when he finally caught up to her.

He grabbed her by the shoulders from behind, shouting her name as she struggled to get away from him, to wade deeper into the sea. "Let me go," she said in a dreamy voice. "Let me go to the sea."

"No, Britta!" He finally scooped her up in his arms, and for a long moment she stared at him with a blank gaze. He saw recognition strike as her features crumpled and she hid her face against his shirt and began to cry. What in the hell was happening? he thought.

He carried her to the car and placed her in the passenger seat, then hurried around to the driver's side and got in. "Are you all right?" he asked, even though he knew it was a stupid question.

Of course she wasn't all right. Something had happened to her, something that terrified him. If he hadn't been there, would she have continued to sink deeper into the water until she'd drowned?

"I don't know what just happened," she said through her tears. She began to shiver uncontrollably, and Ryan didn't know if it was because she was wet and cold or if it was because she was afraid.

"Let's get you home," he said. He started the car and turned on the heater. She cried for just a few more minutes, then stopped and closed her eyes. She continued to shiver even though Ryan had the car heater blowing at full blast.

When they got to the cottage, Ryan led her into the bedroom. She appeared to be in a mild state of shock. She didn't fight him as he helped her out of her wet jeans, nor did she protest when he pulled her blouse off and tucked her in beneath the sheets clad only in her panties and bra. She merely relaxed against the pillow, closed her eyes and appeared to fall asleep.

Ryan sat in a chair next to the bed, staring at her as he tried to figure out what in the hell had just happened. She'd looked as if she was in a daze, a trance of sorts. He sat up straighter. A hypnotic trance.

He thought of what the doctor had told them about the drug that had been injected into her. Stinging Flower, a drug with the properties of strong suggestibility.

Was it possible the person who had abducted Britta had implanted some kind of hypnotic command in her brain? But what kind of a command would make her walk mindlessly into the sea? It didn't make sense, and what didn't make sense worried him.

What worried him even more was that if he hadn't turned away from Ingram Jackson's back door when he had, she might have disappeared altogether in the water and he wouldn't have known what had happened to her.

His heart crashed as he realized how close he'd come to losing her, but along with the clutch of his heart came the pounding questions that had no answers.

He spent most of the day pacing the living room floor, worrying everything around in his mind, wondering if somehow he'd missed a clue that might hold the answer to Britta's missing four days. He checked in with his boss and let him know what was going on.

Britta's abduction and drugging wasn't officially an FBI issue and Ryan knew that what his superior, Kimble Cross, would like most would be for Ryan to remove her from Raven's Cliff and get her relocated someplace else. But Ryan was adamant that he wanted time to chase down this mystery, and Kimble had indulged his wish.

Britta slept until he woke her just after dusk. He'd checked on her several times throughout the day, but her sleep appeared to be deep and without dreams.

It was after seven when he carried in a tray with a bowl of soup, some crackers and one of the diet sodas she liked. He set the tray on the floor next to the bed.

He watched her for a moment, as her features were relaxed and vulnerable with sleep. She had beautiful bone structure and the Scandinavian coloring that made her striking no matter what clothes she wore.

It wasn't just her physical beauty that drew him. She was spirited and bright and had a wry sense of humor that matched his own.

What was happening in that pretty little head? What had somebody done to her mind that would compel her to walk into the sea?

He leaned over and gently touched her shoulder.

"Britta, honey. You need to wake up. You need to eat something." She stirred, a smile curving her lips as she saw him. In that soft, sleepy smile, memories of waking up with her next to him in bed crashed through his head. But when full consciousness hit her, the smile fell away.

As she rose to a sitting position he picked up the tray from the floor and placed it over her lap. "I fixed you some lunch," he said, and tried not to notice the dainty lace bra that barely contained her breasts.

Once again she began to shiver, as if the deep chill that had clutched her before sleep had found her once again. "Eat your soup," he said. "It will warm up your insides."

Dutifully she picked up the spoon. "I don't think I'll ever be warm again," she said. She took a sip of the soup and frowned. "What happened out there, Ryan?"

"I was hoping you could tell me," he replied. He pulled his chair up closer to her side.

She ate another spoonful of soup and shook her head. "All I know is that one minute I was right behind you at Ingram Jackson's back door and the next minute you were pulling me out of the water."

He leaned forward. "And you don't remember why you went into the water?"

"No." She set her spoon down, her eyes hollow as her shivering intensified. She reached out and took Ryan's hand in hers, squeezing tightly. The fear that darkened their beautiful depths tugged at his heart. "What's happening, Ryan? What's happening with me?"

"I don't know, but we're going to figure this out, Britta. I promise you." And he meant it. He was damned if he was going to leave this cursed fishing village until he got the answers he sought.

She shoved the soup away. "I'm just so cold." Her eyes held his appealingly. "Come cuddle with me, Ryan. Get me warm." She tugged on his hand, and even though he knew it was a mistake, he took the tray from the bed and set it on the floor. And even though he knew it was an even bigger mistake, he crawled into bed beside her and pulled the blankets up around them.

As long as he kept his clothes on there shouldn't be any temptation, he thought. He was in control of this situation and he knew he had to be strong.

She trembled against him, and more than anything he wanted to reach inside her and grab that core of ice and melt it so she would finally be warm.

He wanted to take her from this place, from the nightmare that she was now living and put her someplace safe where she would be happy forever. But he couldn't. He was afraid that whatever the destructive force was, it would follow her.

She cuddled closer and laid her hand on his chest, and he wondered if she could feel the thundering of his heart. Although he tried to keep himself rigid and emotionally distant, it was next to impossible with her sexy curves pressed against him and her warm breath on his neck.

He rubbed down her slender back, telling himself all he was attempting to do was get warmth into her blood. But it seemed the only blood that was warming up was his own.

What he didn't want to do was kiss her, yet as she raised her face to his and her lips parted in a silent plea, he was helpless to overcome the rush of desire that swept through him.

He lowered his mouth to hers and tasted her and remembered what her naked body felt like against his, remembered how easily he could lose himself in her sweet warmth.

The one thing they had shared when they'd been together in the past was a passion for each other, and it was that way again. Despite all of his intentions to the contrary, as she opened her mouth to him and wrapped her arms around his neck he was lost.

She flicked her tongue into his mouth, and he deepened the kiss, swirling his tongue with hers. All the questions that had plagued him throughout the day fell out of his head as Britta filled him up. It felt as if they kissed for an eternity and yet it wasn't long enough, would never be long enough.

As if they had a life of their own, his hands wrapped around her back and unfastened her bra. As it fell from her body his hands captured the lush fullness of her breasts, his thumbs grazing her erect nipples.

She moaned, that deep sensual sound that had always touched him on a level no other woman ever had. He wasn't even aware of undressing, nor was he aware of her removing her panties, but suddenly they were skin to skin.

His hands hungrily stroked the length of her, loving the feel of her silken skin. He felt her heartbeat against his own as she arched her hips beneath him, urging him to take her.

Since the moment he'd seen her lying in that clinic bed, he'd had a fever for her, and now he gave in to the sickness of wanting her. Even though he knew she didn't remember making love to him before, someplace inside her the memories must have been held safe for she knew exactly where to touch him, exactly where to kiss him to evoke a desire so hot it burned all rational thought from his head.

BRITTA DIDN'T REMEMBER making love with Ryan before, but her body remembered the touch of his hands, the feel of his skin against her.

His lips moved from her mouth down the slender column of her neck and he captured one of her nipples in his mouth. She tightened her grip on his shoulders as he laved her breast, licking and nipping to bring her pleasure.

"I remember you," she whispered. "I remember your touch. I remember the beat of your heart against mine."

For the first time since she'd come to in the depths of the ocean water, heat fired her insides. She closed her eyes as his mouth moved to her other breast and he sucked and nipped teasingly on the taut tip.

She stroked her hands down his back, loving the play of his sinewy muscles beneath her palms. This was where she belonged. She felt it in her soul, in her very heart. She had no idea what he'd been in her life before, but she knew what she felt at this moment and it was like a homecoming in his arms.

He was hard against her and she reached down and encircled him. The moan that escaped him stirred her desire for him even more and the sound of his pleasure sounded a chord of memory in her head.

She stroked him and he reached down and stopped her, his eyes infernos blazing into hers. He moved between her legs and slowly entered her.

She hissed her pleasure as he went deep inside and she raised her long, slender legs to lock around his back, capturing him in an embrace that stole her breath away.

He moved against her, the exquisite sensations tensing every muscle. Her body trembled, but the tremors that shook her had nothing to do with a cold internal chill but rather the flame of desire that burned inside her.

Teasingly slow, he took her, casting aside all the fear the day had brought, all the uncertainty her life contained at the moment.

She gripped his shoulders and reached up to nip at his neck, wanting to taste his skin as he possessed her. She arched beneath him, meeting him thrust for thrust as they quickly spun out of control.

With frenzied intent they moved together, and she felt the rush of the wave sweeping over her, overwhelming her. With a cry she rode the wave, shuddering and crying against him.

He followed her, softly whispering her name as he tensed against her and went over the edge. He collapsed on top of her, and she buried her face in the hollow of his neck, his heartbeat ragged and quick against her own.

She kept her arms wrapped around his back, hoping to keep him with her all night. She wanted to sleep in his arms, feel him spooned against her throughout the night.

She stroked the back of his neck, his skin warm beneath

her touch. She sighed, the soft sound of a woman sated. She could tell the moment he was about to get up. All his muscles tensed as he raised up on one elbow and gazed down at her. There was something in his expression that took the warm glow out of her heart.

She smiled tentatively. "I'm definitely warm now."

"That was foolish of us," he said, no answering smile on his sober features. "We didn't even use birth control." His jaw muscle throbbed.

"I didn't even think about it," she confessed. "Maybe that was foolish, but I wouldn't take it back. I loved making love with you, Ryan." She ran a hand across his chest. "And if you want to stay here with me for the night I'd gladly make love with you again."

It was absolutely the wrong thing to say. Although his eyes flared with a hint of heat, he rolled completely off her.

"You want the bathroom first?" he asked.

She nodded, and slid out of bed. With complete unself-consciousness she got out of the bed and padded naked to the bathroom.

Once inside she stared at her reflection in the mirror. How she wished she had all the memories of the time they'd shared together before. Perhaps those memories would help her better navigate the crazy emotions she felt for him at this moment.

While she desperately wanted to know what had happened to her when she'd arrived here in Raven's Cliff and mysteriously disappeared, she also wanted to know about the past she'd shared with Ryan. She had a feeling it was far more complicated than what he'd told her.

When she returned to the bedroom, Ryan was on his back staring up at the ceiling. He sat up as she got back into bed.

"I'm going to take a shower," he said. He got up and headed for the bedroom door.

"Are you coming back?" she asked. She wanted him to come back and hold her through the night. She wanted him to keep her nightmares at bay with his solid presence next to her. "I'm still cold, Ryan."

He stopped at the door and turned back to face her, the knot in his jaw pulsing. "Then I'll get you an extra blanket before I go to bed," he said, and disappeared out the door.

She turned over on her back and stared up at the ceiling. Damn her lack of memory. He made her crazy. He was opinionated and stubborn. He had a need to control and he often seemed to intentionally pick fights with her.

But there was still something about him that drew her, not just on a physical level, but on an emotional level, as well. Was it possible that she had feelings for him because while they'd been in Boston he'd been her only contact with the outside world? Somehow she didn't think so.

All she really knew was that making love to him had only confused her more than she'd already been confused. Sooner or later she hoped she'd get back all her memories and would know what it was about Ryan Burton that somehow haunted her soul.

And she'd know what had made her walk into the ocean earlier in the day. She frowned as she thought about that moment when she'd found herself in Ryan's arms, soaking wet and not knowing how she'd gotten there.

It had been one of the most terrifying things she'd ever experienced. The thought of what might have happened if Ryan hadn't seen her walking into the water was even more terrifying.

She'd been half teasing when she'd told him she was cold

again, but now it was true. A deep chill grabbed hold of her as the thoughts whirled around and around in her head.

She got out of bed and turned out the light, then returned and snuggled deeper into the covers. If Ryan didn't spend the night next to her, then she hoped he did bring her an extra blanket because all the "what ifs" that were cascading through her mind had her ice-cold once again.

With a sigh she turned on her side and saw a man staring into the window.

Chapter Eleven

Ryan stood beneath a hot shower spray and cursed himself for his weakness, for his utter stupidity. He'd done exactly what he'd sworn he wouldn't do again. It was unbelievable how easily he'd fallen back into bed with her, despite all his intentions to the contrary.

What's more, she had no idea how tempted he was to get back under the covers with her and fall asleep with her in his arms. But he refused to compound what had already been a monumental mistake.

The same reasons he'd broken off their relationship seven months ago hadn't magically gone away. He was still eleven years older than her. They still argued about everything—from politics to what color of blue the sky was on any particular day.

But most important, he was still afraid that he'd be the kind of husband his father had been, and he wouldn't want to wish that on a woman he hated let alone one that he cared about.

He shut off the water and grabbed the towel on the vanity counter awaiting him. He'd just have to be strong, he thought as he dried off. He'd just have to make sure that it didn't happen again.

As he pulled on his jeans, the piercing sound of Britta's scream came from the bedroom. The sound electrified him and he raced to the bedroom and flipped on the light to see her huddled in the center of the bed, her blue eyes wide with terror.

"A man," she gasped, and pointed toward the window. "There was a man looking in."

"Stay here," Ryan commanded, and raced back out of the room. He grabbed his gun from the coffee table, flipped off the safety and burst out the front door.

Faint light from a three-quarter moon spilled down as his heartbeat slowed and the cold calculation of a soldier took over.

Was it the man who had abducted Britta, the one who had injected her with strange drugs? Had he seen her and Ryan around town and followed them here? Dammit, they should have never put her out there as bait.

Had the shark arrived?

His gaze swept the immediate area and as a shadow near the side of the house moved he pointed his gun. "Freeze or I'll blow your brains out," he said.

"Don't shoot, Burton. It's me." Stepping out of the shadows FBI Agent Michael Kelly appeared.

"Jesus, Kelly," Ryan said irritably as he lowered his gun. "You just about got yourself shot." He drew a deep breath.

"I wasn't sure this was the right place," Kelly said.

Ryan motioned him toward the front door. "Come inside."

Once the two men were back in the house, Ryan pointed the agent toward the kitchen, then went into the bedroom where Britta was still huddled on the bed.

"It's all right," he said to her. "You aren't in any danger, but you might want to get up and get dressed. We have a visitor." He disappeared once again and closed her bedroom door.

Back in the kitchen he found Kelly seated at the table. Ryan supposed most people would find Kelly a handsome man. Tall and on the thin side, he had dark brown hair and blue eyes. He and Ryan had worked together in the past and Ryan had found the man to be both intelligent and friendly.

"What are you doing here?" Ryan asked as he went directly to the cabinet to prepare a pot of coffee. He had a feeling it was going to be another long night.

"Kimble gave me the go-ahead to come out and see if I can help you."

"So, what were you doing sneaking around the house?"

"These bungalows all look alike," he said with an easy smile. "And to be honest, I forgot the address number that Kimble gave me. I was too embarrassed to call him back for it, so I thought if I snooped around a little bit and peeked in a few windows I could find the right place."

How long had he been at the window peeking in? Ryan studied the other man's face carefully but saw no signs that Kelly had seen them making love.

Nobody in the Bureau except Kimble had known the extent of Ryan's previous relationship with Britta. Only Kimble had known that Ryan had been foolish enough to let a professional relationship transform into something personal.

"What's the news from Boston?"

Kelly leaned back in the chair and stretched his long legs out beneath the table. "The Boston Gentlemen are exploding from the inside out. We can't get a handle on exactly what's going on, but with Joey dead they seem to be falling apart."

"Gee, that breaks my heart," Ryan said dryly as he set two cups of coffee on the table, then sat in the chair opposite Kelly.

"How's Britta? Has she remembered anything else about the shoot-out?"

Ryan frowned. "Nothing specific."

At that moment Britta entered the kitchen. She'd dressed in a pair of jeans and a pink T-shirt that enhanced her blond hair and blue eyes. "Britta, this is Michael Kelly, the FBI agent who was responsible for relocating you here."

Michael smiled at her. "Hello, Britta. It's nice to finally meet you."

"Mr. Kelly," she said with a nod as she sat across from him at the table.

"Please, make it Michael," he replied. "And I'm sorry for frightening you. I wasn't positive this was the right place so I thought I'd just peek in the window."

"You definitely made my heart stop for a minute," Britta admitted.

"Michael has come to town to help us figure out what happened to you." Ryan got up and pulled a third cup from the cabinet. "He almost got himself shot lurking around like a Peeping Tom." He poured her a cup of coffee and carried it back to the table and returned to his chair.

Michael grinned. "Thank God you heard me say your name before you pulled the trigger."

Michael reached out and covered one of Britta's hands with his. "Now we can't have people plucking beautiful women off the streets," he said, his voice laced with a flirtatious edge.

All the muscles in Ryan's stomach twisted. He wanted to yell at Kelly, to tell him to stop touching her. Britta pulled her hand out from Kelly's and smiled with a touch of coolness. "We appreciate anything you can do to help," she said.

For the next fifteen minutes Ryan told him everything that had happened since he'd arrived in Raven's Cliff. "I didn't send the gown or the necklace to the lab," he said. "I knew it would be a low priority to get them tested, and that meant it would be months before I got back any results. We've got them in a bag in the bedroom closet."

"Can I see them?" Kelly asked.

"I'll get them," Britta said, and quickly stood from the table.

"She doing okay?" Kelly asked with a frown as she left the room. "She seems kind of distant."

"We've had a rough day," Ryan replied, and told him about her walking into the ocean that morning.

Britta returned with the bag holding the gown and the necklace. She handed it to Ryan as if she wanted no part of touching the items to remove them from the bag.

He pulled them out and handed the gown to Michael, then laid the necklace on the table. Michael looked at the gown carefully. "Hand stitched," he said.

"Yeah, we noticed," Ryan replied.

Michael looked at Britta. "And you were wearing just this when he found you in the lighthouse?"

She nodded. "Just that and the necklace."

Michael carefully folded the gown and placed it back in the bag, then eyed the necklace with interest. "Regular fishing line. In a small fishing village probably everyone owns some."

"You're right. The fishing line is a dead end," Ryan replied.

"It's all so strange," Michael said as he carefully laid the necklace on the gown in the bag.

"This whole town is strange," Ryan replied. He shot a quick glance at Britta, who was sitting back in her chair and twisting a strand of hair while she looked at Michael.

"What made you decide to send me here?" she asked.

"Well, I certainly didn't send you here to be kidnapped, dressed in a gown and let loose in an old abandoned lighthouse." He gave her a charming smile, but his smile fell away when she didn't appear to respond to it. "I saw an ad in a travel magazine for a housekeeper wanted at the Cliffside Inn. I knew you had hotel training and thought it would be a good fit. I figured it was far enough away from Boston and a small enough town that nobody would think to look here. And as far as we know, nobody from the gang has found you here."

Britta nodded, as if satisfied with his answer. She picked up her coffee cup and took a sip, her gaze moving from Michael to Ryan. For just a moment a flicker of warmth filled her eyes, as if she were remembering what they'd just shared.

He broke eye contact with her and looked back at Kelly. He didn't want to think about making love with her. He needed to stay focused and put that behind him. He needed to stay strong to make sure that it would never happen again.

WHEN THE CONVERSATION WENT to other FBI matters, Britta listened absently, her thoughts instead focused on Ryan. She'd seen the true man today, the man behind the facade he presented.

Throughout the afternoon as she'd stayed in bed she'd been aware of him checking on her occasionally. Once he'd pulled the blanket up closer around her neck, then he'd made her soup and brought it to her in bed. His gentle care while she'd been traumatized had shown her more about him than any words he could speak.

Making love with him had been beyond amazing. There had been a sweet familiarity that made her feel as if she were home in his arms, as if that's where she belonged for the rest of her life.

She flushed as she became aware of Michael looking at her expectantly. "I'm sorry, I was distracted."

"Ryan has told me you didn't remember anything about your time in Boston just after the shooting."

"That's true, although I've been getting flashes here and there," she replied.

"She remembers a little bit about the shooting, but not a lot," Ryan said.

"It's slowly coming back to me," she said. "Every day I have a new little snippet of the past that makes its way into my mind."

"That's good," Michael said, then turned once again to Ryan. "I just wish we could figure out what happened during those four missing days."

"She's relatively certain that she was taken by somebody from the gazebo at the inn on the first night she arrived in town, but other than that we haven't learned anything else," Ryan replied, his frustration obvious in his voice.

"Maybe I can dig up something that you two haven't been able to," Michael said. He paused to take a sip of his coffee, then continued, "I'm staying at the Cliffside Inn. Nice place."

"Then you've met Hazel," Britta said.

"Oh, yeah. She's a bit of a kook, isn't she? Did you know she practices Wicca?"

"No, I didn't know that, but somehow it doesn't surprise me," Ryan replied.

"She tells me she's doing all kinds of spells and rituals in an effort to rid the town of an evil curse," Michael said.

Ryan nodded. "The curse of Captain Earl Raven." For the next few minutes he told Michael what they knew about the tragic history and the curse that had gripped the town on the night that Nicholas Sterling III hadn't done his duty and fired up the lighthouse.

When he was finished, Michael laughed. "Ah, a tragic fire, an unexpected hurricane and the legend of an old salty sailor, definitely the stuff that breeds curses." He turned his attention back to Britta. "But I do want to apologize for sending you here. I thought it would be a good fit, but obviously I sent you into some kind of danger."

"It's not your fault. You couldn't know that something bad would happen to me," she said. She didn't blame him for the missing four days. She didn't blame anyone but herself for being foolish enough to go out alone on a fog-shrouded night.

Michael drained his coffee cup and stood. "And speaking of the inn, I should probably get back there. It's getting late."

Ryan and Britta also got up from the table and followed the FBI agent to the door. "What are your plans for tomorrow?" he asked Ryan.

"I'm not sure. I thought we might head out to the docks and ask some more questions there," Ryan replied. "What about you?"

"I may just wander a bit, get a feel for the place. How about I come by around seven tomorrow evening and we can compare notes."

Ryan nodded. "Sounds good."

They said their good-nights and then Michael Kelly left.

"I don't like him," Britta announced.

Ryan looked at her in surprise. "What's not to like?"

"I don't know, it's just a feeling. I especially didn't like it when he touched my hand."

"Maybe subconsciously you blame him for all that's happened to you?" Ryan suggested.

"Maybe." She sank onto the sofa. "Or maybe it's just because I'm still a little shaken up by what happened this morning." And by their lovemaking, she mentally added, but knew now was not the time to explore all her feelings where Ryan was concerned. Nor was it time to tell him that she had every intention of their lovemaking happening again.

"We should probably get to bed. I'd like to start out early in the morning. If we're going to talk to some of the fishermen, then we need to get an early start," Ryan said.

She nodded, stood and started for the bedroom, then paused and looked back at him. "Ryan, sooner or later we're going to have to talk about us, and don't even try to tell me there wasn't an 'us' in the past." She didn't wait for his response, but instead went into the bedroom and closed the door behind her.

It seemed to take her forever to fall asleep, but she awoke before dawn. The scent of coffee riding the air let her know Ryan was already up and about.

A peek out the window let her know it was going to be a dismal day. A thick fog blanketed the earth. She knew it would take hours of sunshine to burn it off, and on most days sunshine was in short supply in Raven's Cliff.

She took a quick shower, and minutes later as she stood before the bathroom mirror drying her hair, a vision unfolded in her mind. She was in the gazebo and a man approached. He was friendly and they exchanged pleasantries. He came closer and suddenly he pressed a cloth against her nose. Then nothing.

The memory was very clear. She could feel the moist warmth of the fog surrounding her and the terrifying pressure of the cloth suffocating her. What she couldn't remember, what she couldn't get a picture of no matter how hard she tried was the man.

She finished drying her hair, then went into the kitchen where Ryan was seated at the table with a cup of coffee before him. "I was abducted from the gazebo that night. It was definitely a man and he covered my nose and mouth with a cloth soaked in chloroform or something like that. I just had a vision while I was standing in the bathroom."

"I don't suppose that vision included the name and address of the man responsible," he said with a touch of wry humor.

"Afraid not." She poured herself a cup of coffee. "In fact, it didn't even give me a picture of the man's face."

"Did you talk to him? Do you think you'd know his voice again if you heard it?"

She joined him at the table and grabbed a strand of her hair and twirled it around her finger. "I know we talked small talk, but I don't remember his voice at all. Isn't that strange?"

"Maybe strange, maybe not." He took a sip of coffee, then placed the cup back on the table. "The doctor told us that one of the properties of the Stinging Flower drug was a high suggestibility."

Britta stared at him as comprehension struck. "So you think maybe this man hypnotized me so I wouldn't remember anything about him."

He shrugged. "It's possible."

She could tell there was something else on his mind. "What are you thinking?" She dropped her hand from her hair and leaned forward in her chair.

"I'm wondering if maybe some other kind of hypnotic command was planted in your head."

"Like what?"

He curved his hands around his cup. "I don't know, but you definitely looked as if you were in a trance yesterday when you walked into the ocean."

"That's a frightening thought," she replied. "Why would somebody plant that kind of command in my brain? For what purpose?"

He leaned back and frowned. "I don't know, it's just one more mystery in a host of mysteries this place has to offer. And speaking of this place, we need to get moving. These fishermen won't remain docked for long."

"Just let me finish my coffee and I'll be ready," she replied.

It was just after seven when they left the cottage. The smokelike miasma still shrouded everything, making visibility difficult.

"I doubt if many fishermen are out this morning," she said.

"They'll be out. They just won't be on their boats. But the minute this fog lifts they'll be sailing. That's why I wanted to get an early start."

It took them only minutes to arrive at the docks where Ryan parked and they got out of the car. Britta fought the impulse to reach for Ryan's hand as the pounding of the waves resounded in her ears and the tangy scent of brine became nearly overwhelming.

The last time she'd been this close to the ocean, she'd walked into it. Why would she have done such a thing? Maybe Ryan was right, maybe somehow a hypnotic command had been planted in her head while she'd been drugged.

As if he read her thoughts, Ryan reached for her hand and closed his fingers around it tightly. She gave him a grateful smile.

Through the veil of the fog she saw a couple of old picnic tables and a group of men seated at them. One of the older men greeted Ryan with a smile. "Well, if it isn't Texas back again and it looks as if you found your lady."

Ryan returned the smile. "That's right. Guess the weather has you grounded this morning, Captain Claybourne." Britta noticed Ryan's Texan drawl had emerged.

"That's a fact," the old man said.

"Hopefully this will burn off by midmorning and we can get out on the water," a younger man replied.

Ryan introduced three of the men to Britta. Captain Claybourne, Sam Lanier and Alex Gibson all made their living from the sea.

"Want to sit for a spell?" Captain Claybourne asked, and scooted over on the splintery bench.

"No, thanks. We're just out here asking some questions about my girl here, Valerie. She seems to be suffering some memory loss and we're just checking to see if anyone remembers seeing her around the area last week. I know I showed you all her picture, but I figured the real thing was better than any photo," Ryan replied.

"I'd remember her if I'd seen her," Captain Claybourne said, his eyes twinkling with good humor.

"You found her, so all's well, right? We have bigger things to worry about," Sam said, his face mournful. "There's talk that people are getting sick and it's the fish we're bringing in making them so."

"Dr. Jamison at the clinic mentioned something about people getting sick," Britta said.

"It's just idle talk," Claybourne said. "Nobody knows for sure what's making those folks ill. You know it's probably one of those foreign flu bugs. Every year there's talk about the Asian flu or the Hong Kong flu. People get sick and that's that."

"It's the curse," the young sailor named Alex said, his voice low. "Captain Earl Raven's curse is going to destroy us all."

The fog seemed to thicken around them and Britta couldn't help the shiver of apprehension that edged through her.

Chapter Twelve

It had been another frustrating day. They'd wandered the streets, going in and out of specialty-food stores and quaint little gift shops. They'd spent an hour in one of the pubs, sipping a beer and hoping for what? An odd look? A gasp of surprise that would identify the guilty?

They had finished up the day by eating dinner at a place called the Cove Café, where the owner had introduced herself as Dorothy Chapman. She'd been a friendly blonde with warm blue eyes and obviously well liked by everyone who'd come into the café.

But ultimately frustration gnawed at Ryan as he unlocked the cottage door and they went inside. As far as he was concerned, this was a useless waste of time. He should forget about Britta's missing four days and just get her settled someplace else.

There was a strong possibility that they would never get answers to the mystery of what had happened to her during those days she couldn't remember.

"Want me to make some coffee?" she asked as they got inside.

"I'd rather have a stiff drink, but yeah, coffee will work."

As she got busy, he threw himself in one of the kitchen

chairs, his mind going over what little information they had. A man had taken her, he'd kept her for four days and injected her with a drug that had probably been locally made. He'd then dressed her in a white gown and a seashell necklace and let her go? Or had she somehow managed to escape her captor and wound up wandering the Beacon Manor lighthouse?

He watched her work, noting the fit of her jeans around her shapely butt, the long legs that had wrapped him close and held him tight. As she turned to face him she offered him one of the smiles that warmed him someplace deep inside, in a place he rarely accessed.

Was it possible he was intent on staying here and attempting to get answers to impossible questions simply to spend more time with her?

Certainly aside from the frustration he felt at not getting any answers to their questions that day, he had to confess to himself that he'd enjoyed the time they'd spent together.

She poured them each a cup of the coffee and sat at the table next to him. "We seem to be spending a lot of time at the table, drinking coffee," she observed.

"Yeah, well, there's not much else to do in the evenings." Ryan checked his watch. "Michael should be here in a few minutes for an update. Maybe he's had more luck at finding answers than we have so far."

She frowned. "I still can't shake that creepy feeling he gave me last night."

Ryan smiled. "Maybe it's because he scared the hell out of you by peeking in the window."

"Maybe," she agreed with a touch of uncertainty in her voice. She took a sip of her coffee, her eyes staring into his with an intensity that made him shift uncomfortably in his chair.

How easily he could fall into those pale blue eyes of hers again. But he couldn't allow himself to do that. He'd been a fool to make the same mistake twice.

Thankfully at that moment there was a knock at the door, and Ryan answered it and ushered Michael inside. Michael greeted Britta then joined them at the table.

"It's interesting. Part of the economy of Raven's Cliff comes from tourism, but I found the locals pretty tight-lipped with strangers," he said. "What little I learned was a bunch of history about the curse and the town. Did you know that the original lens in the lighthouse is constructed of a rare gemstone that supposedly has mystical and healing powers?"

Ryan shook his head. "Nope, didn't know that."

"I also heard that for years on the anniversary of Captain Raven's shipwreck he'd row out and place flowers on the rock where his ship and his family went down. They say that when the lighthouse beam shone on the rocks where his family was lost, people swear they saw the ghosts of his wife and children."

"Everybody loves a good ghost story," Ryan replied.

Michael took a sip of his coffee, then continued, "Have you been out to Beacon Manor?"

"No, we've seen it up on the bluffs, but we haven't been up there," Britta said.

"It's a beautiful place," Michael said. "It's a two-story brick mansion with formal gardens and a pool house and private beach. Must have really been something in its day. Even though you can see some of the damage from the hurricane that hit this area, the house is still amazing. You know it was at one time the home of the bad boy who didn't light the beacon when he was supposed to."

"Nicholas Sterling III," Ryan said.

"Yeah, I've heard conflicting rumors about him. Some believe that he burned to death along with his grandfather the night of the fire. Others think he jumped from the top of the lighthouse and drowned." Michael cocked his head and directed his attention on Britta. "Kind of weird, isn't it, that Nicholas Sterling started the curse by not lighting the lighthouse when he was supposed to and you found Britta wandering the lighthouse?" he said.

"A strange coincidence," Ryan replied, although it was a coincidence that bothered him.

"I also heard that people are getting sick around here," Michael continued.

"We heard the same thing," Britta said. Ryan noticed that her eyes were a pale cool blue as she gazed at Michael. "We haven't met before?" she asked.

Michael frowned. "Not before yesterday. But we did speak on the phone several times to get you set up to come here." He smiled suddenly. "You know how it is, we FBI agents all look alike." His smile fell. "Are you all right?"

Ryan looked at Britta worriedly as she began to twirl a piece of her hair. "I'm just tired," she said, and broke her eye contact with Michael.

"If you don't have any other information, maybe we should call it a night," Ryan said. She did look tired, he thought. The days were beginning to wear on her. If they could just get a break, a lead of some kind to follow.

Michael stood, obviously aware that it was time to leave. "Get some rest, both of you," he said as Ryan walked him to the door. Britta remained at the table.

Michael opened the door but turned back to look at Ryan.

"Have you thought that maybe it's time to get her out of here? She doesn't look so good. Maybe the stress of this whole situation is getting to her. I can have her relocated within a couple of days." He kept his voice low so Britta couldn't hear him.

Ryan hesitated, weighing his personal desire against what was best for Britta. "I still want her here," he finally replied.

He told himself this was what was best for her, that until he understood why she'd walked into the sea the day before he wasn't willing to cut her loose. He needed to know what was going on with her, what had happened to her while she'd been in the clutches of whoever had taken her.

Michael shrugged. "Okay, it's your call for now. Has she remembered anything else?"

"Nothing about the missing time, but she's getting bits and pieces of the shoot-out. I think it's just a matter of time before she remembers everything."

"Good. If she can eventually identify the shooter of our agent, then we'll have new evidence to present and will need her in court again."

"Right now we're just taking things one day at a time," Ryan replied.

Michael grinned. "It's the only way we can take them."

The two men said their goodbyes, and Ryan locked up behind him, then returned to the kitchen where Britta still sat at the table staring out the window where the darkness had become profound.

He saw the strain on her face, the tension that held her shoulders rigid. Maybe it was time to get her out of here. Maybe he was being selfish in keeping her here.

"Michael thought it would be best if we relocate you as soon as possible," he said as he leaned against the doorjamb.

"I don't want to leave here until I know what happened to me," she replied, not taking her gaze from the window.

Her words soothed his conscience somewhat. "You ready to call it a night?" he asked from the doorway.

She turned to look at him, her eyes filled with a light that instantly put him on edge. "No, I'm ready for you to take me into the bedroom and make love to me again."

"I told you that last night was a mistake and it wasn't going to happen again," he replied.

"Why? According to what you told me we were lovers before. You said we both knew the score, that there was no future. We were just wasting time together. Well, I feel like wasting some more time with you again."

Every muscle in his body tensed as she got up from the table and walked toward him. Her sexy rolling-hip walk made every muscle in his body tense.

"What makes you think I'm even interested in making love with you again?" he asked.

"Oh, you're interested," she said with a woman's confidence. Seduction was in her eyes, in the curve of her lips as she smiled at him. "I can tell by the look in your eyes. What are you afraid of, Ryan? You told me it was all good between us before, no harm, no foul, just a fling between two consenting adults."

He wanted to take back the lies he'd told her, lies that had her believing they could have an intimate relationship and nobody would get hurt. He knew better.

Maybe he was being ridiculous in thinking he'd only break her heart again. It was possible when they'd parted before by the next day she'd gotten over the hurt of him saying goodbye.

All these thoughts whirled around in his head as she moved closer…closer still. The familiar scent of her perfume drifted toward him, the floral scent stirring his senses with pleasure.

When she was about to press her body into his, he grabbed her by the shoulders to hold her at bay. "You're right," he conceded. "I want you, but I'm not going to have you again. It ended badly between us before, Britta."

The seduction in her eyes transformed to confusion. "What do you mean?"

He dropped his hands from her shoulders and took a step backward. This was a conversation he'd hoped to never have with her. "When you finally get your memories back you're going to remember that you hated me at the end."

"Why? Why did I hate you?" She gazed at him intently, as if attempting to peer into his very soul.

"Because for those months we were together we lived like husband and wife. We laughed together, ate together and slept together every night. We shared a passion for each other and we acted on it again and again and somehow in the course of that time you fell in love with me." He watched a whisper of pain darken her eyes.

"And you didn't fall in love with me?"

He jammed his hands in his pockets and grinned. "Why, darlin', haven't you figured it out yet? I'm just not the lovin' kind."

"Stop that," she exclaimed with more than a touch of irritation. "Just stop giving me that stupid cowboy act, because I know it's just an act."

He pulled his hands out of his pockets and sighed. "I told you from the very beginning that I wasn't looking for a relationship, but things got out of control between us. You started talking about marriage and babies and a happily-ever-after future, and that's the last thing I wanted in my life. So I left. I had another agent take over your case and I left you. That's the truth, Britta, the whole unvarnished truth. And when you eventually get your memories back, you'd only hate me more for taking advantage of you again this time."

Her face reflected a million emotions and finally settled on a weary acceptance. "I wish I had those memories now," she finally said. "Hating you would make everything so much easier."

She turned and left the kitchen, and a moment later he heard the sound of her bedroom door closing. He released a weary sigh of his own and went into the living room.

He flopped down on the sofa but quickly realized he was too restless to sit. Instead he paced the small room, trying not to think about Britta in bed, Britta in his arms, her body joyously yielding to his.

The scent of her lingered in the air. The bungalow wasn't big enough for him to escape it. Maybe he'd take a walk, clear his head. Hopefully walk off the desire he had to take back his words, to go into the bedroom and crawl into bed with her.

He knocked on her bedroom door. She answered wearing the pale blue silk nightgown that displayed every physical asset she possessed. "I'm going out," he said, trying not to notice the thrust of her breasts against the thin material. "I'll lock up behind me. You have the cell phone handy?"

She nodded. "On my nightstand. Will you be gone long?"

As long as it takes to get you out of my head, he thought. But that would take forever. "No, not long."

"Then I'll just say good-night and I'll see you in the morning," she replied. She closed the door, and he stood for a long moment staring at the wood as a new sweep of desire coursed through him.

He headed for the front door. A headache was trying to take hold in his temples. He stepped out into the night where a faint mist lingered in the air.

Messy. Personal relationships were always messy. He'd learned that lesson very well from his parents. After living through their hell of a marriage, Ryan had never wanted one of his own.

Still, he couldn't help but remember that when they'd been together before and she'd begun to talk about marriage and children, there had been a part of him that had wanted that.

She knew him better than any woman ever had before, and there had been something magical in having somebody who understood his moods, accepted his faults and still loved him. It was when he found himself yearning not just for her, but also for a little boy or a little girl that he truly got scared and ran.

She deserved more than he had to give. He'd done the right thing this time by not allowing anything further to develop between them.

He headed down the street and wondered if his refusal to fall back into a physical relationship with Britta was to save her from more heartache or to save himself?

ALTHOUGH IT WAS relatively early, Britta crawled beneath the covers on the bed and curled up on her side. She'd been in love with Ryan Burton. She wasn't surprised by this piece of new knowledge, in fact, what he'd told her explained a lot of things that she'd been feeling.

From the moment she saw him in the clinic she'd been drawn to him. Somehow, someway her love for him had managed to live inside her heart despite the amnesia that had taken him from her memories.

And he hadn't loved her. He'd just been wasting time with her. Odd, that although she couldn't remember the depth of her love for him at that time, her heart ached with the loss of him.

She had almost made the same mistake again. She realized she was precariously close to falling in love with him one more time.

Despite that silly cowboy chauvinist facade he presented, she could have loved the man beneath. She loved his wicked sense of humor, the tenderness that he had shown her when she'd most needed it. There were a million reasons she could love him, and only one why she shouldn't…he didn't love her back.

And yet there had been moments when she'd seen something shining from his eyes, something that had looked suspiciously like love. There had been moments when she'd felt it in the simplest of his touches.

She squeezed her eyes tightly closed, more confused than she'd ever been. She almost laughed. She had no memory of the past seven months of her life, somebody had abducted her and held her captive for four days and nights while injecting her with a strange drug and all she could think about at the moment was Ryan Burton.

She tried to summon up the hatred that he insisted she'd feel for him once her memories returned, but it was impossible for her to find any ill feelings for him in her heart.

Within minutes sleep reached out to her and she gave in to it, hoping that at least in sleep she would find a little peace from all the emotions that crashed inside her.

She thought it was a dream, the faint scratching sound at

the screen, the soft whoosh of a window rising. She stirred and moved her head against the pillow.

And somebody was on top of her.

She had no chance to scream as sleep was ripped away and hands reached to grab her by the throat. Terror clutched her as her mind grappled with what was happening.

She struggled, trying to kick him, but the blankets that she'd pulled up tight to keep her warm now hampered her efforts.

Big hands grabbed her neck and strangled the scream that she desperately wanted to release. The darkness of the room prevented her from seeing who was on top of her, and his hands squeezed tighter and tighter around her throat.

His weight was heavy on top of her, and she could hear the sound of his rapid breathing, smell the scent of the outdoors that clung to him.

Oh, God. The fear screamed inside her as she realized how much trouble she was in. She needed help. *Ryan,* her mind cried. *Ryan, where are you? Somebody please help me.*

She could scarcely think, as the person on top of her continued to tighten his grip around her neck. She punched him in the sides with her fists and twisted her head back and forth in an effort to dislodge his hold on her, but a darkness that had nothing to do with the night edged closer.

It was like her nightmare about being in the sea. She felt herself sinking, going deep into the depths. For just a moment there was a peaceful sensation of floating, of all her worries and cares drifting away.

But then she realized she couldn't breathe and was being held beneath the depths against her will. She could hear the pounding of her heartbeat in her ears as it became impossible to draw a lungful of air. Help me. The words swirled around in her head.

Her pummeling of his sides slowed as an exhaustion she'd never felt before overwhelmed her. Her arms and legs were like lead weights, impossible to lift or move.

Her vision grayed, and someplace in the back of her mind she realized she was going to die. This man was going to kill her by squeezing the air out of her.

The thought of death shot a new panic through her and with a final tremendous effort she reached up her hand and scratched at the man's face. As her fingernails found skin she raked as hard as she could.

The man hissed a curse and loosened his grip on her neck just enough for her to release the scream that had been trapped inside her.

"Britta?"

As if she were under water Ryan's voice sounded very far away. The man on top of her jumped up and crashed out of the open window.

With a sob Britta sat up just as Ryan burst open the bedroom door and flipped on the light. She pointed to the window. "A man," she managed to gasp as she grabbed her throat. "He tried to strangle me."

Ryan flew back out of the room as Britta rubbed her aching neck and gulped in big breaths of air. If Ryan hadn't come in when he had, she would be dead. There was no question that the man had intended to squeeze her neck until she was no longer alive. And he'd nearly succeeded.

On wobbly legs she got up from the bed and pulled her robe around her, then walked over to the window where the screen had been cut away to allow entry. She crashed the window closed and locked it.

As it banged shut a kaleidoscope of colors and action

whirled through her head. Memories cascaded, tumbling one over the other as they presented themselves in her mind.

She could see herself and Ryan in bed, a navy blanket tossed carelessly to the side as they ate pepperoni pizza after having made love. She saw his head thrown back in laughter, his eyes gleaming with wicked light as he reached for her.

Scenes of times they'd spent together flashed like a slide show. The two of them together in the shower, at a dining-room table and curled up on the sofa with a bowl of popcorn between them.

The scenes snapped and crackled in her mind, then the slides changed from Ryan to the Woodlands Hotel in Boston and that fateful night.

Autumn leaves spread out in colorful array on a marble fireplace mantel. Pumpkins and squash in an artful display. Massive floral arrangements in reds, golds and oranges sprawled across tabletops.

She walked out of her office, her feet sinking into the lush carpeting. As she entered the large hotel lobby she saw the men standing here and there around the room. Thick tension filled the air. Lights sparked off the barrel of a gun.

Shots fired. Smoke in the air. Blood. God, so much blood. She hid behind a chair and watched in horror as her little world exploded apart by the violence taking place.

The young FBI agent with blond hair and blue eyes motioned for her to stay down, then as she watched in horror his chest blossomed crimson and he fell.

Britta gasped in stunned surprise as in her mind she saw the face of his killer.

"I couldn't find anyone." Ryan spoke from just behind her. "Are you all right? Did he hurt you?"

She turned to face him, a hand at her burning throat. "I remember."

He holstered his gun and grabbed her by the arm. "Come away from the window." He pulled her into the living room and there he looked at her neck, and his eyes narrowed, as he suddenly pulled her to his broad chest and muttered a curse.

She melted against him, thinking of those seconds when she thought she was going to die. She would never have felt his arms around her again. She would never have had a chance for any kind of future with or without him.

He took her by the shoulders and gently moved her away from him, his gaze looking at her intently. "Are you sure you're all right? You want something to drink? Maybe a cool cloth?" He released her altogether, his features taut with tension.

"No, I'm okay now." She sank to the sofa, her legs still shaking. He remained standing as if he weren't quite sure what to do with himself.

"Did you see who it was?"

"No, it was too dark in the room. But I'm pretty sure I know who it was."

He finally sat next to her. "Who?"

"Michael Kelly."

Ryan stared at her in surprise. "Why would Kelly try to kill you?"

"Because he's afraid I'll remember that he killed that FBI agent in the hotel that night. I remember, Ryan. I remember everything. It all came flashing back just a few minutes ago."

He frowned. "Kelly?" he said softly, as if wanting to make certain he'd heard her correctly. "Was it an accident? I mean, in the melee of all the gunfire, did Kelly mistakenly kill the wrong man?"

She reached up and grabbed her hair and began to twirl it furiously around her finger. "It was no mistake. He pointed his gun right at the agent and pulled the trigger and then he ran away." She dropped her hand from her hair. "It should be easy to find out if I'm right about him trying to kill me tonight. I scratched his face. I think I scratched it hard enough that the marks should show for at least a couple of days."

She dropped her hand and instead entwined her fingers on her lap. "That's why I didn't like him when I first met him," she said. "He gave me a bad feeling, and even though I didn't specifically remember him, somewhere inside I recognized his evil."

Ryan leaned back against the cushion, his astonishment still on his features. "That explains why so many of our sting operations went awry, because somebody was tipping off the boys in the Boston Gentlemen. We knew it had to be somebody on the inside, but nobody ever suspected Kelly."

"I'd stand up in a court of law and swear to what I saw that night, and what I saw was Kelly shooting a fellow agent in cold blood."

Ryan offered her a tight smile. "You might have to stand up in court and testify once again. What about the missing four days? Do you remember anything about them?"

"No, nothing about them," she replied. She rubbed a hand across her still-stinging throat. "Do you think he had something to do with those days?"

Ryan sat up straight and frowned thoughtfully. "It doesn't feel right that he did. If he was worried about you identifying him then why would he keep you alive if he'd abducted you? Why would he inject you with the drug? No, he wouldn't have taken you off someplace. He would have just put a bullet in your head."

She scooted closer to him on the sofa. "Do you think maybe it was a gunshot we heard that day as we were walking away from the inn? Do you think maybe he was already in town and tried to kill me then?"

"I don't know." His voice was hard. "But eventually we'll find out." He reached out and touched her bruised throat, his features dangerous and his eyes glinting with a hard light. "I could kill him for doing that to you."

She pushed his hand away and instead threw herself into his arms as the realization of what she'd just been through hit home. She began to cry.

He tightened his arms around her, holding tight as the terror of the attack shuttered through her. She hid her face in the hollow of his throat as she thought of those moments when she was certain that death had come to claim her.

Sobs ripped through her, and he comforted her by stroking down the length of her back, crooning to her in a soft tone. "It's all going to be okay, Britta," he said. "I swear to you, everything is going to be just fine."

She knew he meant well but it was a lie. Nothing was ever going to be just fine again. For along with the memories of the shoot-out had come the memories of her intense love for the man who held her now.

And along with the memories of love came the ache and grief at losing him.

Chapter Thirteen

It was a long night. Once Britta stopped crying and calmed down, he got her settled with a blanket on the sofa, where she fell into an exhausted sleep.

He didn't want her in the bedroom out of his view. He didn't intend to take his eyes off her until Kelly was behind bars. Now that he knew what the man was capable of, his blood ran cold.

How many times could he assure Britta that everything was going to be all right? How many times could he say the same words to her over and over again before they became just empty promises?

As she slept soundly, he got on the phone. The first call he made was to Kelly's cell phone. Ryan didn't expect the man to answer, and he didn't. Instead it went directly to voice mail. "Kelly, it's me, Burton. You aren't going to believe what just happened here at the bungalow," Ryan said. "Somebody cut the screen and opened the window and got into Britta's bedroom. Whoever it was tried to strangle her. It was too dark for Britta to see who it was, and I checked out the area but didn't see anyone. Anyway, I just thought I'd give you a heads-up. Call me when you get this message. I think maybe whoever had her for those four days tried to get her again tonight."

Ryan clicked off. What he hoped was that his message would give Kelly a false sense of safety that would keep him at least for a while not only in town but also at the inn.

What he'd like to do was hunt the man down and make him pay for the death of their fellow agent, make him pay for what he'd done to Britta.

Kelly had all the knowledge in the world on how to make a person disappear. Working with the Witness Protection Program was part of his job. He arranged false identities and new lives for people who needed them. There was no reason he couldn't do it for himself.

It was important that he be picked up as soon as possible, while he didn't know that Britta had regained her memory of the shoot-out in Boston, while he thought he was still safe.

For much of the remainder of the night, Ryan was on the phone, speaking to his superiors, letting them know what had occurred and that Britta had identified one of their own as a rogue agent.

He had to tell his story half a dozen times, then he requested information as to Agent Kelly's whereabouts on the days that Britta had gone missing and on the morning that he'd thought they'd dodged a bullet.

It didn't take long for him to have some of the answers. He'd been satisfied to learn that there was no way Kelly was responsible for the four days of Britta's disappearance while she'd been here in Raven's Cliff.

However on the day that Ryan had thought a bullet had been shot at them, nobody could verify Kelly's whereabouts. Thank God the bullet hadn't found its mark.

By the time he'd finished the calls, he slumped into the chair opposite the sofa, exhausted but unable to sleep. It was always sad to realize one of the good guys had become one of the bad.

He suspected that Kelly had walked the wrong path, and the motive had probably been money. There had been many times in Ryan's career that he could have taken a bribe and looked the other way, but he'd never been a lover of the things that money could buy.

Maybe it came from the fact that as a young boy he'd learned not to get too attached to things. Things got broken when war broke out, houses and apartments were lost when eviction papers were served.

Maybe that's also why he had never formed a deep attachment to any person. He stared at the woman sleeping on the sofa. Except Britta. Her loving heart and spirit had somehow reached inside him and grabbed hold of what little innocence, what little love had survived his parents' marriage.

It was near dawn when he finally fell asleep in the chair next to the sofa, his gun within easy reach and his dozing senses still on the alert for any danger that might come their way.

He awoke two hours later to find Britta still sleeping. He stared at her for a long time, grateful that her sleep seemed to be deep and peaceful.

Despite the tears she'd shed the night before, he considered her one of the strongest women he'd ever met. He was aware that part of his love for her was built on a fierce admiration. She'd had everything she knew and treasured ripped away from her in a single night, and yet during the time he'd spent with her in Boston she'd met each loss with a stoic acceptance.

As he remained watching her, she began to stir, first stretching like a cat with her arms overhead, then opening her eyes.

For an unguarded moment they looked at each other, and

all of what they'd shared in the past was there, both the joy and the pain.

He broke the eye contact and stood. "Good morning," he said. "How are you feeling?"

Her slender hand moved to her discolored throat and she nodded. "Okay, I think. Better than last night." She sat up and ran a hand through her sleep-tousled hair. "Anything new?"

"Why don't I go make the coffee, you get dressed and then we'll talk," he replied. It was far too difficult to concentrate with her in that skimpy nightgown.

Minutes later she joined him at the kitchen table where he had the coffee ready and had toasted some English muffins.

She was dressed in jeans and a pale blue turtleneck that perfectly matched her eyes and hid the marks Kelly had left on her neck.

"Sometime today Kelly will be picked up and taken back to headquarters," he said as she slid into a chair. "I had him checked out as far as the dates of your abduction here were concerned, and it's impossible that he had anything to do with it."

"What about the day we thought we were shot at?"

"That's still up in the air. My gut feeling is that he was probably responsible for that, but not the days you were gone."

"So we still have a mystery on our hands." She reached for one of the English muffins and looked out the window where dawn was just beginning to break. In the distance the lighthouse was visible, one of the first structures to catch the early-morning sun. At the very top the damage from the fire that had occurred so long ago was visible.

"What are our plans for the day?" she asked as she turned to look at him once again. Her eyes were as blue as the morning sky outside the window.

"We're going to just sit tight here until I hear that Kelly is in custody." He reached for an English muffin. "There's no point in going out and making ourselves a target for him."

"Good, then I want to talk about us."

Her words hung in the air between them as Ryan tensed. This was what he'd dreaded all night when she'd told him all her memories had come back.

"If all your memories have returned to you, then you should know we have nothing to talk about," he said.

"But I think we do." She paused, and once again her gaze went out the window. For a long moment she was silent, as if collecting her thoughts.

Her silence made his dread grow deeper. He knew he didn't want to have this conversation with her, that it would probably mirror the last talk they'd had more than two months ago when he'd walked out of her life. He'd never forgotten the pain that had darkened her beautiful eyes, and he'd never wanted to see that kind of pain on her face again.

He steeled himself as she returned her gaze to him. "I love you, Ryan. I loved you before and I'm in love with you now."

Each word was like an arrow into his heart, piercing him with a sadness he'd only known once before, when he'd initially told her goodbye.

"And I think you loved me before and that you love me still," she said. As usual, with her emotion came her accent. Under any other circumstances he would have found it charming, but not now. He didn't want to hear the emotion in her voice. He didn't want to see it raw and naked as it shone from her eyes.

He drew a weary sigh. "Britta, why do you want to rehash the past? Hopefully within days we'll be done here and you'll move on to your future somewhere else with somebody else."

"I don't want to move on with somebody else," she protested. "I didn't understand why you walked away from me the first time, and I'll understand even less if you walk away from me again."

She reached across the table and covered his hand with hers. "We're good together, Ryan. We have laughter and we have passion. I don't care what you tell me. We were in love. You can't lie about it any longer. I have my memories back and I know what happened."

He pulled his hand from beneath hers, finding her very touch like fire against his skin. He got up from the table and instead stood rigid and straight. "We also fought."

She frowned at him. "We didn't fight," she protested. "We discussed things. We had different points of view. That's not fighting, that's exchanging ideas."

"Yeah, we exchange ideas and it isn't long before somebody gets angry and then voices get louder and tempers flare and before you know it the police are at the door for domestic violence." The words bubbled out of him unbidden, his voice harsh and angry, and he wasn't sure who was more surprised by them, him or her.

"Ryan." She got up from the table and approached him where he stood, a look of confusion on her face. "Ryan, what are you talking about?" Her voice was soft as a caress and touched him despite the bad visions the talk had evoked in his head.

He wanted to run from the conversation, from the childhood memories that had become nightmares he had as an adult. But he knew she wouldn't let him run, that she wouldn't be satisfied until he gave her answers.

"That's what love and marriage mean to me," he finally

said. "Fights that turn into thrown fists, screaming matches that always ended in a police presence at my house." The words spewed out of someplace deep inside him. He had never talked about his childhood to anyone before in his entire life, had always found the topic too painful, too intimate to share.

"I spent most of my childhood hiding in the bottom of a closet afraid that when I finally came out one or both of my parents would be dead, killed by each other. We moved from place to place, evicted by landlords after so many disturbance calls to the police. My parents said they loved each other, but that didn't stop them from their fighting. I decided then I'd never get married, that I didn't want to have anything to do with love."

"But that's not love," she said, her voice soft and winsome. She took a step toward him but stopped as he narrowed his eyes and held up a hand, wanting to keep her away from him.

"Why didn't you ever tell me all this before?" she asked, her eyes filled with a deep compassion.

He didn't answer and she did exactly what he hadn't wanted her to do, she touched him. She not only touched him but she wrapped him in her arms.

He stood stiffly in her embrace, not wanting to yield to her softness, to the promise of something different that he saw in her eyes, that he felt in her heart beating against his.

"Love is about allowing for differences in people, it's about loving them despite the fact that they think differently or have another opinion. We argued, yes. I'm a strong woman and I have my own opinions and I like to be heard. You're the same way. We argued in a healthy way, Ryan, and never crossed that line. What your parents had, that wasn't about love. That was about control or something else, but it definitely wasn't about love."

He could have stood in the sweet embrace of her arms forever. He might have even fallen into the fantasy of possibility her words produced, but at that moment his cell phone rang from his pocket.

She dropped her arms from around him as he reached for the phone. "Burton," he said.

He listened to the caller on the other end and looked everywhere in the kitchen but at Britta. Thank God for the interruption, otherwise he might have lost the last modicum of strength he had to keep her at an emotional distance. And that would have been a mistake for both of them.

He finished the call and hung up. "Kelly is now in custody. The arrest went smoothly without conflict. He confessed to everything. He was on the Boston Gentleman payroll. He took the shot at us in the town square and he's sporting a nasty scratch down the side of his face. He is hoping to cut a deal by offering information about the gang, but we aren't going to deal with him. He'll be facing a murder charge, attempted murder concerning the attack last night and a host of other charges that will keep him in prison for a very long time."

"That's good news," she said, her eyes still shadowed with emotion.

"That's great news. In fact, I think we should go out for breakfast to celebrate." He wanted to get her out of the bungalow, out among other people, where having a personal conversation would be impossible. "Then we'll hit the streets again. Maybe today we'll learn something that will move us closer to ending all this."

He didn't look at her, but instead turned and walked into the living room, aware of her following just behind him. "I'll shower first," he said as he grabbed some clean clothes from his suitcase. All he wanted to do was escape before she could begin a dialogue again.

She remained silent as he disappeared into the bathroom, but he had a feeling the personal issues between them weren't resolved as far as she was concerned.

As far as he was concerned they were done. Tonight after she went to bed he was going to call and request that somebody else be put in charge of her care.

It had been a mistake for him to come back into her life in any capacity, and he intended to do exactly what he'd done the first time he'd gotten in over his head with her...run.

As USUAL by the time Britta and Ryan left the bungalow the early-morning sunshine had disappeared and dark clouds hung low in the sky, creating a gray pall that clung to everything. But the gray weather outside couldn't compete with the utter bleakness of Britta's heart.

The mystery of the missing four days of her life couldn't compare with the mystery of why Ryan refused to give their love any chance at all. Her heart had ached for him when he'd told her about his parents' marriage and the terrible childhood he'd suffered, but if there was one thing Britta had learned over the past seven months it was that you couldn't do anything to change your past but you could pick the path of your future.

It was obvious he was done with any further conversation about their relationship. Since they'd left the cottage he'd been closed off, so distant she had a feeling nothing she said would reach him, so she didn't even try.

She almost wished for her amnesia back so she wouldn't remember the pain of losing him before, a pain she knew, if she couldn't change his mind, she'd experience all over again.

They headed for the docks where they'd discovered a little diner that offered terrific breakfast fare. It was obviously a favorite place of the local fishermen, and today several of them sat at the counter or lingered around the wooden tables.

Ryan lifted a hand in greeting as he saw Sam Lanier and Captain Claybourne seated at one of the tables. Captain Claybourne motioned for Ryan and her to join them.

Britta would have preferred that she and Ryan sit by themselves, but Ryan beelined to the table as if glad for the company.

"You're both out and about early this morning," Captain Claybourne said as they sat at the table.

"I figured most of you would be out on the water already," Ryan replied.

"Weatherman says a front will be blowing in sometime this morning with high winds and rain. No use going out just to come back in," Claybourne said.

At that moment the waitress arrived to take orders. When she'd left the table the men made small talk. They spoke about the unusually bad weather, about local politics and sports. Britta listened absently, her attention focused on Ryan's handsome features.

Had she fallen in love with him simply because of their forced proximity? They'd been cooped up together in a small apartment in Boston for months while they waited for the trial to begin. It had been a forced intimacy that was unnatural. Except it hadn't taken long for it to feel completely natural.

No, she hadn't fallen in love with him simply because they'd lived together like husband and wife for several months. She hadn't fallen in love with him because he'd been convenient and the only male in sight.

She'd fallen in love with him because of his inner strength

and convictions, his moral code that mirrored her own. She'd fallen in love with him because he hated to lose at card games and loved crime dramas on television. She loved him because he had a wonderful ability to laugh at himself and could make her laugh no matter what her mood.

Who knew why two people fell in love with each other? It was one of the great mysteries of life that nobody could completely figure out.

When the waitress refilled their coffee cups, then left the table, Britta focused on the conversation instead of dwelling on thoughts of Ryan.

"People are getting nervous," Captain Claybourne said. "The entire town is on edge. Look around in here. This is usually a noisy crowd, fishermen telling tales, flirting with the waitresses, tourists taking in the local flavor and such."

Britta realized there was an unnatural hush in the diner. Men sat alone at the counter, huddled over coffee as if trying to get warm. Men and women at the tables spoke in low, hushed tones as if sharing secrets as their gazes furtively darted first one way, then another. Beneath it all was a thrum of energy that felt discordant and sick.

"Are you a superstitious man, Captain Claybourne?" Britta asked, looking at the salty old fisherman curiously.

His weather-worn features softened with a smile. "As a rule most sailors are a superstitious lot. Never begin a voyage on a Friday, never rename your boat or you'll incur the wrath of Neptune. Whistling on board is said to bring on a storm and avoid black cats and overturned washbasins before getting on a ship. That's just a few, but I could go on and on."

"Please don't," Sam said with a laugh. "If you get him started, we'll be here until midnight." He cupped his hands around his mug of coffee. "People are whispering that the curse of Captain Earl Raven has taken over the village, that evil walks the streets now."

Ryan looked at Captain Claybourne. "You born and raised here, Captain?"

He nodded. "That's the truth."

"So you were here the night the Beacon Manor lighthouse burned."

"And rode out the hurricane that followed," Claybourne replied. "Hell of a night it was. The whole town saw the lighthouse on fire. It would have been worse if the storm hadn't moved in and the rain hadn't doused it."

His eyes narrowed and he paused to take a sip of his coffee. "The storm that night was the likes of which I'd never seen before. It was as if hell had come up for a visit. The next morning the town was damaged, the lighthouse was burned and that poor woman from New York was gone."

"Woman from New York?" Britta asked.

"She was a rich one engaged to Nicholas Sterling III," Sam said. "A real looker, too. Her father was some millionaire businessman. She seemed quite smitten with Nicholas." He frowned. "Now that one, a trust-fund fellow, thought his family's money could solve any problem that might come up." Sam frowned. "He should have lit the lighthouse that night. It was the anniversary of Captain Raven's wreck. The lighthouse was supposed to shine on those rocks where the old sailor had lost his family.

"After that night, Nicholas's father lost everything, made some bad investments and eventually left town a broken man," Claybourne continued. "There's still a lot of storm damage around, but we've slowly been rebuilding."

Sam snorted. "It would help if the mayor kept his promises. Of course, I know right now he's grieving the loss of his daughter. But we've been hearing him talk about tearing down the damaged buildings and cottages for years and it hasn't been done."

"What do you think about Chief Patrick Swanson?" Ryan asked the men.

Sam grinned. "The man scares the hell out of me."

"He's a good man," Claybourne said. "Tough but protective of the town and his men."

At that moment the waitress delivered their orders and they focused on the food. As more people came in for breakfast there was still a pall over the occupants. Even the clink of silverware and glasses seemed subdued.

They had just finished the meal when a woman came flying in the door. She was a birdlike older woman, thin and with dark hair as wild as Medusa. Her body shook as she looked around the room. She froze as her frantic gaze landed on Sam Lanier.

"Sam Lanier!" she cried in a strong voice that was at odds with her petite stature. She rushed toward the table with purposeful strides, and as she got closer her dark eyes filled with tears.

"Mabel, what's wrong?" Sam rose, his sun-browned face looking worried.

"I'll tell you what's wrong. I cooked up that nice piece of fish you dropped off to me the other night and I fed it to my Jimmy. Now he's in the clinic bad sick and they're saying it might be the fish." A sob tore from her throat as she jabbed a finger in Sam's chest. "You give me bad fish to feed my husband? How could you do such a thing?"

There wasn't a sound in the diner. The other patrons had

stopped eating when she'd first called Sam's name, and the silence was palpable.

"The doctor said he could die, Sam. What have you done? What have you done?" she said as tears once again streaked down her face.

The waitress hurried over and placed her arm around the sobbing woman's shoulder. "Come on, Mabel, let's go in the back and talk."

As the waitress led the distraught woman from the room, Sam sank back into his chair, looking shell-shocked. "She and her husband are my neighbors. We've been good friends for years." He fumbled in his pocket and pulled out a wad of money. He pulled off several bills and threw them on the table, then stood. "I've got to get over to the clinic and see Jimmy."

As he hurried out of the diner, Captain Claybourne curled his meaty hands around his coffee mug. "Bad times ahead," he muttered more to himself than to Britta or Ryan. "I feel it in my bones—there's bad times ahead."

As if to punctuate his sentence an explosive rumble of thunder clapped overhead.

Chapter Fourteen

Moments later Ryan and Britta left the diner. Although the sky lit up with lightning and thunder crashed, not a drop of rain fell from the sky. The wind blew like a banshee, shrieking around buildings like something from another world.

"We'd better just head back to the cottage," Ryan said, half yelling to be heard.

Britta nodded her agreement, the storm filling her with a terrible feeling of portent. Like a malevolent whisper in her ear, like an icy finger pressed at the base of her spine, an inexplicable terror gripped her as they ran beneath the ever-darkening skies.

They reached home just as the rain began to fall, pelting the windows like tiny bullets. Britta stood at the window and stared out, trying to still the horrible presentiment that held her in its clutches.

It had to be the storm, she told herself, or maybe it was the talk of a mysterious fever sweeping through the town. Or perhaps it had been the ominous words of Captain Claybourne. But no matter what the reason, she couldn't shake the overwhelming feeling of doom. She was afraid and she wasn't sure why.

She turned from the window to see Ryan seated on the sofa,

looking irritated and as on edge as she felt. "I finally realize what you meant when you said this town is sick," she said as she sank into the chair opposite the sofa. "I feel it now." She wrapped her arms around herself, chilled to the bone. "It was in the air in the diner—a thick, almost palpable tension."

"I've felt it since I stood up on that bluff at the wedding and watched Camille Wells go over the edge," he replied.

"Do you think the fish is what's making people sick?"

"Who knows? It's possible it's just a virus of some kind making the rounds." He got up as if too restless to sit and began to pace the length of the small room. "I know it sounds crazy, but I feel as if my guts are twisted inside out, like something is about to explode."

"Something did explode," she replied. "That poor woman. I guess it was easier to blame Sam's fish than face the possibility that the doctor doesn't know what's going on with her husband. But I know what you're talking about. I feel a pressure inside me." She sighed and touched her tender neck, fighting another deep chill as she thought of Michael Kelly's hands around her neck. "Maybe it's just because I'm not used to somebody sneaking into my bedroom and trying to strangle me."

Ryan smiled tightly. "At least we don't have to worry about him anymore."

She watched him, and the heartache she'd been fighting since they'd had their talk that morning began to press against her chest. Maybe her bad feeling had nothing to do with anything other than the fact that she knew eventually she'd have to tell Ryan goodbye…again.

To her surprise, tears stung her eyes. She tried to blink them away, but they refused to be controlled. As they oozed down her cheeks she realized they were the result of the combination of both fear and pain. The inexplicable fear she couldn't place, but the pain in her heart sat directly at Ryan's feet.

"I'm going to the bedroom," she managed to say as she stumbled to her feet. "I'm…I'm not feeling very well."

She ran for the bedroom door and closed it behind her, then threw herself across the bed as her tears came faster. Suddenly she was crying for everything that had happened over the past almost eight months of her life.

She'd had to give up her dream job and the apartment that she had lovingly furnished piece by piece. The entire first twenty-five years of her life all had to be forgotten, packed away and transformed because she'd been at the wrong place at the wrong time.

And if that wasn't enough, after all that had been taken from her, she'd fallen in love with a man who was unable to love her back in the way she wanted. He'd left her and she'd wound up here, in this village damned by a curse and having to lose the man who held her heart all over again.

She knew life wasn't fair. She'd learned that fact when her parents, good and loving people, had been taken from her far too early. Yes, she knew life wasn't fair, but she seemed to be taking more than her fair share of hard knocks lately.

"Britta?" Ryan knocked softly on the door. "Are you all right?"

"No," she cried, the word catching with a new sob. "Go away."

Of course, because he was the most perverse man on the face of the earth, he did no such thing. Instead he opened the door and came into the bedroom.

"Why are you crying?"

"Because I feel like it," she replied with a touch of aggravation. She certainly wasn't going to tell him she was crying over him. She was only willing to give up so much of her pride.

At that moment thunder rattled the windows and she had a flash of someplace strange, someplace that had the faint smell of gas and oil and seashell necklaces hanging from hooks. Night and then day, a weight around her ankle.

She shot up from the bed and gasped as she felt the evil surrounding her. There must have been something on her face, for Ryan was instantly by her side as she began to shake uncontrollably.

"Britta, what is it?" He sat on the edge of the bed and placed his hands on her shoulders.

"Necklaces hanging on hooks, seashell necklaces, some of them completed and some of them still needing to be strung. I saw them in my mind and I smelled oil and fish and I'm so scared." She frowned and tried to cling to the vision. "There's something around my ankle and I can't move. Footfalls coming. There's something evil out there and I think it wants me."

She shivered against him and he pulled her into his arms. "Do you remember anything else?" he asked as his hand stroked down her trembling back.

She shook her head against his chest. "No, just that." She squeezed her eyes tightly closed, as if to will away any more of the terrifying images. "I'm afraid, Ryan. I've never been as afraid as I am at this moment. I don't know whether it's the storm or what Captain Claybourne said or the snippet of memory I just got, but I'm terrified." She began to sob in earnest.

"Britta, honey, don't cry." He pulled her into his arms and she wanted to stay there forever. She was safe here, in the shelter of his strong embrace. "Baby, you know I can't stand it when you cry."

She raised her head and looked at him and saw what shone from his eyes. Love. It was there in the green depths, raw and naked for her to see.

"You love me. I know you do. Ryan, don't let me go again," she cried. "Can't you see that we belong together?" She clung to him as he tried to back away from her. Pride be damned. She had to give it one last shot. She knew that time was running out. She felt it in her heart, the ticking of the clock that would take him away from her forever.

"It doesn't matter how we feel about each other, Britta. We're like oil and water together."

"We aren't," she protested, and looked at him in frustration. "Sometimes I feel as if you intentionally pick fights with me, and now you're using that as a weapon against me. I'm not your mother," she said. "And you aren't your father. Their mistakes won't be ours. Don't you see that?"

He managed to extricate himself and he stood. "I'm not willing to take that chance," he said, his voice deep and low with emotion.

"We talked about building a family, about having children together. You said you wanted that. We both wanted that."

"It was a fantasy," he retorted. "It was just a stupid fantasy we made up for a little while. I don't believe in curses, Britta. And I don't believe in fantasies. I'm just not willing to change my life by inviting anyone in."

"Then you're a coward," she said angrily. She got up from the bed to face him. "You're allowing the misery of your past to dictate your future. Your parents screwed up your childhood and now you're letting them screw up the rest of your life. You were foolish enough to walk away from our love once before. Please, don't be a fool again."

For a moment she thought he would yield. There was such a deep yearning in his eyes she thought finally he would grab hold of her and the love they had between them, but he straightened his shoulders and backed toward the bedroom door.

"Last night I talked to my supervisor and we both agreed it would be best if I am pulled off this case. Sometime in the next forty-eight hours a new agent will be arriving to take my place." His voice was harsh, then softened. "It's for the best, Britta. It's for the best for both of us."

"Don't tell me what's best for me," she said with a touch of bitterness. "You'd take a bullet for me, but you won't take a chance on my love. Just get out," she said wearily, and was grateful that he did what she asked. He left the room and shut down her heart as he closed the door behind him.

SHE REMAINED in the bedroom for most of the day, and Ryan found himself sitting on the sofa as rain continued to bombard the windows and her words played and replayed in his mind.

As a frightened child he'd made the vow never to marry, and in all his years as an adult, nobody he'd met had been able to change his mind.

Britta had been the only woman in his life who had made him wonder what it would be like to share a life with her, to share a future. He'd never been as happy as he'd been during the months he'd shared with her, but he believed in his heart that it had been nothing more than a fantasy spun by time and place.

He didn't know how to be a husband. He sure as hell didn't know what it took to have a good marriage. She'd been right about one thing. He had consciously picked fights with her, pushed all her hot buttons to keep her at a distance. Unfortunately, it hadn't worked.

She was also right about something else—he was a coward. He'd rather lose her now than invest months…even years and then have her leave him. It was easier for him to break her heart now than to risk his own being broken later.

It was just after five o'clock when the rain stopped and the sun began to peek around the last of the dark clouds. Hunger drove him into the kitchen and he was seated at the table and eating a sandwich when Britta came out of her room, obviously driven by hunger, too.

She looked as tired as he felt, drained from the emotional warfare that had gone on between them. She nodded to him as she padded across the floor to the refrigerator. He didn't say anything to her, but rather waited for her to speak.

She made herself a sandwich, grabbed a can of her diet drink and then joined him at the table. "It looks as if the storm is moving away," she finally said, breaking the silence between them.

The skies were clearing, but his heart remained dismal and gray. "Yeah, looks like it," he agreed. It had always amazed him, her ability to let go of a fight after it happened. During the previous time they'd spent together, he'd learned that she was a woman who didn't hold a grudge, that once the arguing was over and she was certain that he'd heard what she was saying, she was through.

She took a bite of her sandwich and chewed and looked out the window where the sun slanted down at odd angles from the partly cloudy sky.

"Do you know who they're going to send here to protect me?" She finally looked at him and her gaze was neutral, not displaying any kind of emotion at all.

"Sorry, I don't."

"He probably won't care about the missing four days of my life, will he?"

Ryan frowned. "No," he answered truthfully. "I think probably he'll just begin the process to get you relocated, unless you want to stay here."

Once again she peered out the window and a slight tremor shook her body. "No, not here, that's all I've decided for certain."

"Britta, earlier you said something about a place with the seashell necklaces hanging from hooks and the smell of oil. Have any other flashes of memory come back to you?" If there was one thing he'd like to do before he left here, it was to solve the mystery of those missing four days of her life.

He didn't feel right leaving that question unanswered and knew that her new handler would just want to get her settled in a new place as quickly as possible.

In fact, Ryan had known that his supervisor had only been indulging him in allowing them to stay here in Raven's Cliff for as long as they had. But Ryan didn't like unsolved mysteries. Part of the reason he'd joined the FBI was because he liked solving puzzles.

"No, nothing else," she replied. She picked up a chip from her plate and munched it with a crunch. "But I haven't been trying to think of it."

"Concentrate and tell me again what you remembered."

She frowned and her hand reached up to twirl her hair. "I saw shell necklaces like the one I was wearing when you found me. They were hanging on hooks."

"And where were the hooks?"

"In the wall, a rough-hewn wooden wall." She looked at him in surprise.

"Keep focused." He pushed the plate with the last of his

sandwich aside. "Was the wall painted? Anything specific about the wall?"

Her frown deepened and she shook her head, her finger twirling her hair faster. "No, it was just a wall."

"And what about the smells? Tell me again."

"Gasoline...oil...fish." She dropped her hand from her hair and sighed in frustration. "That's all. I can't remember anything else."

He leaned back in his chair and worked it around in his mind. "Is it possible you were being held on a boat?"

She tilted her head to one side, the warm sunshine drifting in the window and playing on her hair, the side of her lovely face. "I don't know. I guess maybe it's possible. But, I don't remember any rocking motion or the sound of an engine, but that doesn't mean it wasn't a boat." She dropped her hand from her hair. "There are still a lot of things I just don't remember."

Ryan thought of all the fishermen he'd met over the past couple of weeks. Certainly they were a colorful bunch of men, but was it possible one of them was a weirdo who abducted women for some nefarious purpose? Or maybe she hadn't been on a boat at all. For all he knew, the guilty man could be a butcher, a baker, a candlestick maker.

The fact that in her flash of memory she'd seen several necklaces worried him. Why have that many necklaces if you didn't intend to put them around the neck of another unsuspecting victim?

What in the hell was going on in Raven's Cliff? The mayor certainly seemed to have secrets, the fish were too big to believe and a mysterious illness was sweeping through town. A bride had been blown off a bluff, and an unknown assailant had abducted Britta for an equally unknown reason.

"I've never been a big believer in curses before," he said, "but I have a feeling if I stayed around here long enough, I'd believe."

"It's like there's a veil of something bad that covers the whole town," she said thoughtfully. "Even when the sun does finally shine, it's like it can't quite penetrate the shadows." She gave a small laugh. "I sound more than a little half-crazy."

"No, not at all," he protested. He was just grateful she was talking to him, that at least for the moment there was no emotional baggage between them. "I know exactly what you're saying."

"By nature I'm hot-blooded and rarely get cold, but from the moment I woke up in the clinic I've had a chill deep inside me that just won't go away, and I don't think it's just a result of whatever happened to me while I was here. It's something in the air."

"You won't have to worry about it for too much longer," he said. He'd decided he would encourage the new agent that arrived to get her out of here as soon as possible. She was more emotionally fragile than he'd ever seen her.

"But what about the strange spells I get? Like walking into the ocean that day we went to find Ingram Jackson?"

"I'm hoping that once we get you away from here, whatever it is will pass." There was no question that the fugue states she fell into worried him, but there was nothing they could do except hope that time and distance would solve that issue.

"Maybe I should definitely decide to relocate to a desert area where there's no water for me to walk into," she said.

For the next few minutes they ate in silence. Although there was no overt tension between them, a sadness emanated from her and he knew that he was at least partially responsible for that sadness.

"I just want you to be happy, Britta. I want you to get settled someplace new where you never have to be afraid again and you can build a happy life for yourself."

"I know that, but I can't help that my heart is aching," she said, the evidence of that ache darkening the blue of her eyes.

"It will pass," he replied. "Eventually this time with me will be nothing more than an old bad dream. You'll forget all about it."

She smiled sadly. "You misunderstand, Ryan. Oh, sure, my heart is broken, but the real sadness I feel is for you. Eventually I probably will go on and love again, although I can't imagine that it will ever be as strong, as real as what I feel for you. But you've closed yourself off and will never know true love, true happiness, and that makes me want to cry for you."

Her words haunted him later that night as he settled down on the sofa. He was exhausted because he'd only had a couple of hours' rest the night before, but sleep didn't come easily.

Was he taking a little boy's fear and allowing it to dictate the life of a man? Nobody who hadn't lived through domestic abuse could understand the deep scars it left on the children, scars that he'd carried into his manhood.

Was it a mistake to walk away from Britta and the love she offered with such open arms, such a passionate heart? Maybe he was the biggest fool on the planet.

He thought of Camille Wells, who had been on the verge of tying her life with the handsome assistant district attorney, Grant Bridges, only to be blown off the bluff before taking her vows.

She'd reached out for her future happiness, and fate had intervened. It didn't seem fair that Ryan's happiness was only a door away, and yet he refused to grasp it, to grasp her with both hands.

He drifted off to sleep with his heart heavy and the uncertain feeling that somehow with Britta he'd made a horrible mistake.

It was sometime later when his eyes snapped open. He was instantly awake and alert. His hand snaked out to grab the butt of his gun. Something had awakened him, a sound that didn't belong in the dead of night. But what had it been? What had pulled him from his sleep?

He remained perfectly still, muscles tensed as he waited to identify what exactly had awakened him. A noise came from Britta's room, then he heard the faint squeak of her bedroom door opening.

His muscles relaxed. Maybe she was thirsty and was going to the kitchen for a drink of water. Nothing indicated to him that she was in any kind of trouble.

He was just about to close his eyes once again when she walked into the living room. The tension that had just begun to ebb away coiled tight inside him as he saw her in the faint spill of moonlight coming from the window.

Clad in the white gauze gown and with the seashell necklace around her neck, she looked like a wraith he'd dreamed up.

Chapter Fifteen

"Britta?" he said softly.

She gave no indication that she'd heard him. She paused a moment and cocked her head to one side but didn't appear to be aware of his presence. Her bare feet padded against the tiled floor as she headed for the front door.

Ryan hurriedly sat up and grabbed his jeans. He called her name again as he stood and pulled on his pants, then reached for his T-shirt and yanked it over his head. By the time he had his shoes on she'd unlocked the front door and opened it.

As she stepped out into the night where faint moonlight played on the low-lying fog that cloaked the small town, Ryan tried to decide what to do.

Should he wake her? His first instinct was to grab her by the shoulders and shake her until her eyes became focused and he knew she was fully awake and out of the control of whatever had her in its grip.

But another part of him whispered that he should wait and watch and see what she did next. It was obvious she was in one of her fugue states, and as she slipped out the door it was also obvious that she was moving with a sense of purpose.

If he woke her now he might never know what this was all

about. He decided to wait, to shadow her movements and see where she was going. He'd stay close enough to keep her safe from harm, but he'd allow her to play out whatever was in her drug-addled mind.

She headed down the street and he followed, gun in hand as his gaze swept the area for any imminent danger. The fog seemed to create an unnatural silence.

The streets were still, the cottages dark as the occupants slept. The vapor in the air gave the night an otherworldly appearance, but Ryan kept his focus on the woman in front of him.

The air was close, oppressive and the scents of brine and decaying fish were stronger than he'd ever smelled. The fog seemed to be thickening. As if it had a life of its own it swirled around in the air with what appeared to be ominous intent.

Ryan frowned and mentally shook himself for such fanciful notions. *Just stay focused on Britta,* he told himself. *Keep her safe above all else.* He didn't sense anyone else in the area, didn't feel the creepy sensation of somebody watching them from the shadows or hidden in the fog. Still, he kept his gaze darting from Britta to either side of the sidewalk, afraid of what might suddenly rush out of the darkness.

She didn't appear to notice the sidewalk beneath her bare feet and she moved with that jerky, marionettelike walk, as if she were not the one controlling her movements. He had no idea where she was headed, but there was no hesitation in her step.

He could hear his own heartbeat pounding in his ears as he easily kept four or five paces behind her. It was as if he and Britta were the last people on the face of the earth. No dogs barked, no cars came by, it was just the two of them and the fog that felt like an eerie warm moist breath on his bare skin.

They walked for what seemed like an eternity. Her pace never varied. Slow and steady, she didn't look left or right, but kept going like a toy with an endless supply of battery power.

Ryan suddenly realized where she was headed. The lighthouse. A shaft of moonlight found an empty space in the clouds and gleamed down like a spotlight on the structure, the light exposing the fire-ravaged upper deck.

Why would she be going there? Ryan tightened his grip on the handle of his gun as a terrible sense of foreboding gripped him. She was going back to where he'd found her, dressed as she had been on that night.

And when she arrived, what would she do? What was the ultimate command that might have been planted into her brain by some sick twist?

A wind picked up, billowing the folds of her gown and making her look like a ghostly apparition. A chill walked up Ryan's spine.

Although Ryan didn't consider himself a superstitious man, he was a man who believed in instincts and intuition, and at the moment, even though there was nothing concrete to explain his feelings, he felt as if the very air was rife with evil.

His hand grew sweaty on the butt of the gun and panic stabbed him when, for just a moment, Britta disappeared in a thick bank of fog. He picked up his pace, breathing a sigh of relief when he caught sight of her again.

He felt as if it had been an eternity since they'd walked out of the bungalow door, but a glance at the luminous dial of his watch let him know they had been walking for about seventeen minutes. It was now one-thirty, the time when she should be sound asleep in her bed.

As they drew closer to the lighthouse, her pace began to

pick up. She stumbled once and nearly fell, but righted herself as if pulled upward by the strings of a puppeteer.

Stop her, an inner voice whispered. Still, he followed, closer now to her, close enough that he could hear her labored breathing.

The low thrum of panic that had filled him since he'd awakened and seen her standing there in the dirty, gauzy gown and seashell necklace now grew louder and more intense.

Stop her! The voice grew louder in his head. *Stop her before it's too late.* But too late for what? Too late for who?

"Britta?" He called her name, his voice sounding oddly muffled as if the fog were a sound barrier and only he could hear himself.

She didn't falter.

It was only when they reached the shore below the lighthouse that the panic became too big to contain, that he knew he had to stop her. She was heading directly for the waves that crashed and spewed as the wind picked up in force.

"Britta!" He shouted her name and hurried to catch up with her.

She broke into a run, as if someplace in her mind she knew he wanted to stop her from whatever she was compelled to do.

"Britta, stop!" He managed to grab her by the arm. She jerked away from him and stumbled to one knee. She jumped up and ran toward the water.

Ryan followed and grabbed her by the shoulders and spun her around. "Britta, for God's sake," he cried as she fought to escape his grasp. "Stop it. Wake up!"

This time was different. When she'd fallen into one of these states before he'd snapped her out of it by merely calling her name. But even with his hands firmly on her shoulders and with him screaming in her face, she stared at him with blank, dead eyes.

"I must go," she said, her features contorted in frustration. She tried to twist away from him, but he held on tight, knowing he was probably bruising her shoulders by his firm grip, but not caring.

"Go where? Where do you need to go?" he asked.

"To the sea. I need to go to the sea." Her voice was now a pleasant singsong that iced his very heart, his very soul.

"Why? Why do you need to go to the sea?"

"Please, I must go. It's what I need to do." With surprising strength she jerked her shoulders and almost got away from him once again.

They were close enough to the water's edge that he could feel the spray from the waves, smell the scent of rotting seaweed and fish. He feared that if she got away from him again, she'd be in the water before he could stop her. Something drastic had to be done.

Hoping that she'd forgive him, he raised his hand and slapped her hard across the cheek. She hissed in a breath and stood perfectly still.

She raised a hand to her cheek, the blankness in her gaze ebbing away as she stared up at him.

"Ryan?" His name was a half sob from her lips just before she fainted to the ground.

SHE WAS IN THE SEA, embraced by the water that held her in its loving arms. This was where she was supposed to be. It was her destiny. The water was warm, and for a moment she felt safe and protected as she rocked with the waves.

Then the watery arms that cradled her began to rock her

back and forth more forcefully. The water surrounding her grew cold, like an icy wind blowing from an Arctic front, and panic took hold of her.

Her face hurt. Her cheek. And her feet. What on earth had she done to her feet? Then she was aware of the gritty feel of sand and rock beneath her and Ryan calling her name over and over again.

She surfaced from the depths to find herself in his arms on a shore near the lighthouse. And in the resurfacing, she remembered.

Flashes went off in her head like lightbulbs popping and exploding. Image after image crashed through her head. She wrapped her arms around Ryan's neck, surprised to realize he was saying her name over and over again.

"It's okay. I'm okay," she said, and held tight to him. Finally she slowly sat up. She was surprised to find herself in the gown and necklace, equally shocked to realize they were on the beach below the Beacon Manor lighthouse.

"How did I get here?"

"We walked," he replied.

"That explains my aching bare feet," she said. She raised a hand to her burning cheek.

"I slapped you. I'm sorry. I didn't know what else to do. I couldn't get you awake and you were going to walk into the ocean." Even in the dim light she could see the worry in his eyes as he held her hand firmly in his. "Are you sure you're okay?"

She nodded. "But I remember. Oh, God, Ryan, I remember everything." Her head filled with the chilling images of the four days she'd endured. She struggled to get to her feet, and Ryan quickly stood and helped her up. "We need to call

Patrick Swanson," she said. "He needs to know what I remember." She felt sick and she swayed, unsteady on her feet.

Ryan scooped her up into his arms. "We'll call him from the bungalow. I want you inside where it's safe." He began walking.

He asked no questions of her as he carried her home and she was grateful for that. She kept her arms curled tightly around his neck and her head buried in the crook of his neck as he took long, fast strides through the mist.

He held her almost painfully tight, as if afraid she might jump out of his arms and disappear into the thickening mist. But she didn't mind his arms so tight around her.

When they finally reached the bungalow, he carried her inside and to the sofa, then disappeared into the bathroom where he got a warm washcloth and a basin of water then knelt at her feet.

"What do you remember?" he asked as he gently cleaned off the bottoms of her feet.

She winced as he worked the cloth against the tender skin. "I remember the place where he took me, and we need to find that place, Ryan. It's important. You need to call Chief Swanson and get him here."

He finished wiping her feet, then sat back on his haunches. "Do you know who took you?"

She searched the memories that now filled her head. "No, I can't get a picture of him on the night that he took me from the gazebo, and I don't remember seeing him at the place where I was held." She stood, a bit shaky on her feet. "While you call Patrick, I'm going to go change clothes." She plucked at the gown. "I need to get this off me as soon as possible."

As she went into the bedroom, she heard Ryan calling Swanson. Her fingers trembled as she took off the necklace that circled her bruised neck. The shells were warm in her hand, as if they had a life of their own. She threw it on the floor, not wanting to touch it another minute.

She then pulled off the gown and tossed it to the floor, grateful to get it away from her skin. She redressed in a pair of jeans and a pale blue lightweight sweater. She needed the warmth of the sweater as a new chill took possession of her body.

Wrapping her arms around herself, she stared at the gown and necklace on the floor, knowing that somehow they were part of a ritual of some kind, a twisted, sick ritual that had almost had her as a leading character.

She returned to the living room where Ryan awaited her. "Patrick will be here in a few minutes." He patted the sofa next to him.

She sat, and immediately he pulled her close to him, as if he knew she needed his warmth, his strength to go back in time to those missing days.

"I'm not going to ask you any more questions until Patrick gets here," Ryan said. "I only want you to have to go back there once."

"Thanks, I appreciate it," she said, and snuggled closer against him, her love for him casting some of the chill away. "I think maybe I won't have to worry about the hypnotic commands that were implanted in my head anymore. I think the return of my memory means the drug is finally out of my system."

He tightened his arm around her, nearly squeezing the air from her. "I hope you're right. I don't ever want to go through a night like this again. When you passed out on the beach, I thought I'd lost you forever."

A knock fell on the door, and almost reluctantly, Ryan untangled himself from her and got up to answer. Patrick

Swanson walked in along with a man he introduced as Officer Brent Matthews.

For the first ten minutes of the conversation Ryan laid it all on the line, telling the two about Britta's real name, that she'd been located here because she'd been a material witness against Boston Gentlemen gangsters and that Michael Kelly had tried to kill her. He explained that Kelly was now in FBI custody and would no longer be bothering anyone in the town of Raven's Cliff.

Patrick listened intently as Ryan went on to explain to him about what had happened tonight, how Britta had dressed in the gown and necklace and walked to the beach near the lighthouse, determined to lose herself to the sea.

"It was obvious she was in some kind of a trance," Ryan said. "We think the trances are a residual effect of the drug she was injected with."

"This Stinging Flower stuff," Officer Matthews said.

Ryan nodded. "As far as we can tell, this is some sort of homegrown drug. There's nothing whatsoever about it in the FBI database."

"So, you were in a trance," Patrick said, his gaze on Britta. "Then what happened?"

"I slapped her to bring her around," Ryan said with an apologetic glance at Britta.

"And when he did, all the memories of those four days came back to me," she said, finally speaking for the first time. "I was abducted by a man from the Cliffside Inn's gazebo the first night that I arrived in town." She frowned thoughtfully. "I can't tell you who did it. Things are a bit fuzzy, but I know he put a cloth over my nose and mouth and I fell unconscious."

The chill inside her was back, seeping into her very bones,

walking icy feelings up her spine. "When I came to I was in a room on a cot. My hands were tied together and one of my ankles was chained to the wall."

She shivered as she remembered that moment of awaking, of realizing she was in danger yet unable to help herself. She'd tried to get loose, working her hands to escape the rope, pulling the chain to dislodge it from the wall, but she'd been unsuccessful. The worst part was not knowing who had her and why.

"The windows were boarded up, but I knew it was day when I first woke up. I could see light around the boards. I was alone that day, then I heard his footsteps coming, and by then it was night. I remember him coming into the room," she continued, grateful when Ryan grabbed her hand and squeezed it tightly. "He gave me a shot, and things get fuzzy after that."

"Did you know who he was?" Patrick asked.

"No, and I know it sounds strange but I have no memory of what he looks like," she replied. "I can't seem to get a visual picture of his face."

"We think maybe the drug he injected into her, along with a hypnotic suggestion, erased her memory of his identity," Ryan said.

"But I do remember the place where he held me," she added.

"What did it look like," Officer Matthews asked.

"The walls were wood and it smelled like oil and gas. I think it was some kind of a boat place."

"That doesn't exactly narrow things down," Patrick replied. "This town is filled with boat places. We've got covered docks, boat storage, boat repair…the list goes on and on."

She closed her eyes, willing herself to seek details that

might help them identify the place. "There were necklaces hanging on hooks, and material for the gowns in one corner." She sat up straighter on the sofa. "There was a workbench on one side. And there was a picture of an old sailboat painted on the wall. It was faded and chipped...and there was a letter *J* there, too." She opened her eyes once again.

"That sounds like Jay's place," Officer Matthews said.

"Jay's place?" Ryan looked from Matthews to Patrick.

"Jay's Motor Repair. It's down by the docks. Been closed up since the hurricane five years ago. He had an old clipper painted on the wall inside his work area."

"You have to go there," Britta said, and jumped up from the sofa. "We all have to go there."

There was a burning urgency inside her. She knew something, and it was vital that Chief Swanson know it, too, but she couldn't put her finger on it. "We have to go there," she repeated. "I have to show you."

"Britta, we should stay here, let Patrick and Officer Matthews check it out," Ryan protested. "You've been through enough tonight."

"No," she replied firmly. "I have to go. There's something there I need you to understand. I can't explain it, but I have to be there."

Patrick's hazel eyes held her gaze intently. "Okay, let's go."

"We'll follow you in my car," Ryan said.

Within minutes they were headed out. Fog still swirled like a living, breathing entity, threatening to envelop the cars and making driving difficult.

"You let me know if you start feeling weird or anything," Ryan said as he cast her a worried glance.

"Don't worry, you'll be the first to know," she replied.

"Trust me, I don't intend to drift far from your side." She frowned. "I don't know what it is, but I just know there's something in the place that's important I show Patrick, that's important he know."

"But you aren't sure what it is now."

She shook her head and sighed in frustration.

Thankfully they didn't have too far to drive. Within minutes they pulled up in front of a building that sat on a large piece of property.

Patrick parked with his headlights beaming on the structure and Britta stared at it. Weathered to a deep gray, the wooden building looked as if it wouldn't take much of a wind to blow it to the ground. She had no memory of being here, but that didn't mean much. She would have been brought here unconscious and had been in one of the strange trances when she'd left.

They got out of the vehicles and Patrick grabbed a couple of strong-beamed flashlights from the truck. Matthews had his own flashlight so Patrick handed Ryan the extra one.

Patrick shone his light beam on the front of the building, where a wooden sign hung crookedly and creaked in the wind. It read Jay's Motor Repair.

"Is this the place?" he asked Britta.

"I don't know. I don't think I ever saw the outside of the building. I won't know for sure until we get inside." Her heartbeat raced as she thought of going in, of seeing the place that had haunted her dreams.

"As far as I know, the place has been abandoned since Jay left town after the storm," Patrick said.

It was possible it wasn't the right place, Britta thought, although she desperately wanted it to be. The urgency that had filled her all day long now screamed inside her.

All three men pulled their weapons as they cautiously approached the front door. "Stay back," Ryan said to Britta, and made sure she was behind him. "Stay back until we know it's secure."

She stayed two steps behind as they walked up the three steps to the door. The flashlight beams barely cut through the thick fog that surrounded them.

"It's padlocked," Patrick said when he reached the door.

"Brent, get a crowbar from my trunk," he instructed. As Officer Matthews hurried back to the car Patrick shone his light on the lock. "Can't imagine why anyone would want to lock up a dump like this."

"He had to lock it," Britta said. "He didn't want anyone to accidentally stumble inside and discover his lair."

"Boards on the window, just like you said," Patrick said to Britta. "Makes it impossible for us to peek in and have a look around."

Matthews returned with the crowbar, and he and Patrick managed to pull the lock right off the rotten wood. Britta's heartbeat accelerated as Patrick pulled on the door and it opened with a creak. The hairs on her nape stood up as she anticipated what they would find inside.

Ryan grabbed her hand and allowed the two policemen to enter first. "You still doing okay?" he asked.

"I'm fine," she assured him with a tight smile.

"Clear," Patrick called from inside.

Ryan squeezed her hand, and the two of them entered.

"We tried the lights. They don't work," Patrick said, his face a ghostly mask as Ryan's flashlight found it.

She could smell the faint odor of gasoline and motor oil, that familiar scent that tightened her stomach. As Ryan shone his light around the space, she followed it with her eyes and gasped as it hit the wall where seashell necklaces hung from hooks.

This was it. The place where she'd spent her missing four days. A wooden worktable was just beneath it, holding spools of fishing line, a small portable drill and dozens of shells.

"I was here," she said, tears burning at her eyes. "This is where he held me." The room now smelled of madness, for surely it was madness that had been in here with her. A madman had sat at that workbench and strung seashells into necklaces. A madman had sewn the gown that she would wear as she walked into the sea.

"Call in some men. We have a crime scene here," Patrick ordered Matthews. "And we need light. Make sure somebody brings a couple of floodlights."

As Matthews once again disappeared to do his chief's bidding, Ryan placed an arm around Britta's shoulders. "Don't touch anything," he said to her softly.

She forced a smile to her lips. "Don't worry, we used to watch all those crime dramas together, so I know not to touch anything in a crime scene."

Patrick walked over to where they stood, a deep frown on his features as his bald head gleamed brightly in the flashlight beam. "I owe you an apology," he said to Britta. "I wasn't sure I believed your story that day you two came to my office to talk to me."

"It's all right," Britta replied. "I'm not sure I would have believed my story, either." She leaned closer to Ryan.

"This is just bizarre," Patrick said. "Lately it seems as if there're too many bizarre things going on in this town. I don't like it. I don't like it at all." He sighed. "We might as well go outside and wait for my men and those lights to arrive."

The three of them stepped back outside, and Britta sank down on one of the steps, Ryan sitting next to her as Patrick walked toward his car.

"You okay?" Ryan asked.

She smiled at him. "Aren't you getting tired of asking that?"

"I can't help but be worried. You want to go back to the house?"

"No. I still need to be here. I told you there's something here, something important." She frowned. "I'm not sure what it is, but maybe with brighter lights inside I'll know."

It took almost an hour for more officers to arrive and the floodlights to be put into place. Britta and Ryan sat in his car and out of the way of the officers as they went about their work.

Both Ryan and Britta napped off and on as they waited. They talked little, both exhausted by the events of the night.

It was almost dawn when the evidence gathering was complete and Patrick indicated they could go back inside. "The only fingerprints we managed to pull were around the cot area and those are probably yours from what you told us," he said, his frustration obvious. "The prints are small like a female's.

"I want this guy. I can't be having women taken off the streets in my town." He eyed Britta with a piercing gaze. "You think of anything, no matter how small the detail, that might lead me to this guy, you let me know." He frowned. "I don't have much hope that anything we bagged and tagged is going to help us identify this creep."

Britta nodded and stepped back inside the building with Ryan and Patrick at her heels. "There's something here," she said thoughtfully. With the aid of the brilliant floodlights, she wandered the room wanting, needing to find whatever it was that nagged at her.

The necklaces had all been bagged up and taken away, as had all the items on the workbench. She stared at the cot, remembering the terror in the moments that she'd been conscious.

"He kept me pretty drugged," she said, more to herself than to the others as she wandered the room. "But there was something he said…something he showed me that is important." She felt a whisper in her ear, a cold evil breath on the side of her face. "He told me something. He didn't speak much, but he told me something important."

The two men said nothing. They simply stood by the door and allowed her to wander the room. The sense of urgency she'd felt upon arriving hadn't waned in the hours that she and Ryan had waited to get back inside.

Then she saw it. What had been nagging at her, the important information she knew she needed to show Patrick, to tell him.

"Here," she said as she pointed to the wall. About two inches above the workbench a set of numbers were scribbled in pencil.

Patrick frowned and moved closer. "We saw those, but we didn't know if they had been written by the man who held you or by Jay or somebody else years ago."

"He wrote them. The man who had me," she said. Again she remembered a faint whisper in her ear and an icy hand gripped her heart. "They're coordinates."

"Coordinates to what?" Ryan asked.

She stared up at Patrick. "It's the coordinates to another one. That's what I needed to tell you. That's what was so important." She grabbed hold of Patrick's strong forearm. "I wasn't the first," she whispered. "Oh, my God, I wasn't his first."

Chapter Sixteen

The moment the sun rose high enough in the sky to start the search, the boats went out, armed with both professional divers and the coordinates taken off the wall.

Britta and Ryan stood on the beach with a growing crowd of people as the news rippled through the sleepy little town that a body was buried at sea.

The sun had quickly dispersed the last of the heavy fog that had shrouded the town the night before, and the sky was the perfect blue of a perfect Maine day, but it wasn't a perfect day. It was a day of death. The only thing they didn't know was whose grave the coordinates marked.

Ryan had tried to talk Britta into going home to get some much-needed sleep, but she'd been adamant that she needed to be here. She'd spoken little throughout the long hours of the night as they'd waited for dawn to break, but she seemed to be finally at peace.

Chief Swanson stood nearby, in contact with the men on the boats through his phone. He paced the sand, stopping occasionally to stare out to where the boats were barely visible in the distance.

Ryan had been impressed by the lawman throughout the

long night and the morning. He'd watched as Swanson had delegated responsibilities to his men, coordinated the search party and asked Britta question after question in an effort to glean any additional clues.

For some reason Ryan had thought that once Britta got back all her memories, his uneasy feeling about Raven's Cliff would disappear, but that wasn't the case.

As he stood on the shoreline in the bright early-morning light he still felt the aura of evil surrounding them, as if it had dark arms around the sleepy fishing village and refused to let go.

He stared out at the lighthouse not too far away. Were the strange events going on in the town the result of a ghost from the past? Had Captain Earl Raven been a benevolent spirit watching over the town until the night somebody had not followed his command?

"Ryan…Valerie," a familiar voice called from behind them. He turned to see Hazel Baker hurrying toward them. Clad in a bright orange caftan with flowing sleeves and wearing sparkly gold sandals, she stumbled hurriedly across the sand to where they stood.

"I heard they're looking for something," she said. "A victim of the man who had you." She looked at Britta, and her lips trembled with emotion just before she suddenly threw herself at Britta and gave her a hug. "You poor dear. How on earth did you ever get away?"

"It's one of the few things I don't remember," Britta said as Hazel released her. Throughout the night in the brief conversations Ryan and Britta had shared, they'd speculated on how she had come to be wandering the lighthouse when he'd found her. But she'd had no real memories of how she'd gotten away from her captor.

Hazel looked at Ryan, her eyes dark and without their usual good humor. "It's the curse. I just know it is. I've felt the bad times coming for weeks now. I've cast spells and lit candles and asked the Goddess to protect us, but I fear the strength of Captain Raven's curse is too strong."

A new chill filled Ryan as he realized the woman was feeling exactly what he'd been feeling, that some indefinable evil had found its home in Raven's Cliff. Britta moved closer to him, as if the chill of malevolence infected her, too.

A stir went up in the crowd nearest the shore. Patrick walked over to them, a grim expression on his face. "The divers have found something. They're in the process of bringing it up."

The ever-growing crowd of people buzzed with curious energy. As the sun drifted higher in the sky, the humidity built, becoming oppressive and cloying as they waited for the boats to return.

A speedboat came to shore and picked up Patrick, then carried him to the bigger boat out in the water. Britta grabbed Ryan's hand, her expression strained as she followed the progress of the speedboat.

He wasn't sure how she was still standing under her own steam. The night had been endless, and Ryan was certainly feeling the result of too little sleep. His eyes felt grainy and raw, and his entire body ached with his exhaustion.

He smiled at her and touched her cheek. "You amaze me," he said softly. "You are so strong."

There was sadness in her eyes as she returned his smile. "I just wish whoever is out there had been strong enough to overwhelm the monster."

They remained standing on the beach until the speedboat

brought Patrick back and he disembarked. He walked toward them, his face weary and his shoulders slumped just a bit. The crowd grew somber, a respectful silence descending on them all.

He pulled Ryan and Britta to the side, away from the other people. "The divers found her. There wasn't much left, but I think it's Rebecca Johnson. DNA testing will probably confirm my suspicions."

"That's the woman you thought was lost in the hurricane, right? Nicholas Sterling's fiancée?" Ryan asked.

"Yeah, well, no hurricane dressed her in a white gown and a seashell necklace, tied her to the bottom of a rowboat and then sank that boat with concrete blocks and old anchors," Patrick said.

Ryan felt a sickness in the pit of his stomach as he imagined what the young woman had endured before her death. Who was responsible?

Patrick placed a meaty hand on Britta's shoulder. "You were one lucky lady. If you hadn't escaped when you did, we might have been dragging your body up from the depths."

He glanced over their shoulders. "There's Mayor Wells. I need to go fill him in and tell him it looks as if we have some kind of creepy serial killer on our hands. And tell him it's not his daughter we've found."

At that moment Ryan realized how close he'd come to losing Britta. What if he'd slept so soundly that she'd walked right past him and out the front door? Had the killer been waiting for her that night in the shadows? Hidden in the fog? Waiting to take her to a boat and tie her in, then weigh it down and cast her to the depths of the sea?

He turned to look at her, but she was looking over his shoulder where Patrick Swanson and the mayor were in conversation.

The mayor was dressed in a suit that Ryan would bet cost a month of Ryan's salary. Again he thought of that moment at the wedding when he'd seen money exchange hands and the odd phone conversation he'd overheard.

The mayor nodded and with Swanson approached Britta and Ryan. "I was wondering if maybe you knew anything about my daughter," he said to Britta. "You know, she went missing off the bluff. I just thought maybe…you might…"

"How dare you come here?" Britta exclaimed, her voice filled with venom.

Ryan frowned and placed a hand on Britta's arm, but she shook it off and took a step closer to Perry Wells. "You're the devil who brought the evil to the sea. It's all your fault. You hear me, it's all your fault."

Mayor Wells stumbled backward, his features displaying first a look of surprise and then what Ryan thought was a hint of guilt. "Young lady, you're obviously distraught," he said. He looked from Ryan to Patrick, then muttered about business that needed to be taken care of and turned on his heels and stalked up the beach.

Britta expelled a deep breath and stared at Ryan in horror. "I don't know why I said that. I have no idea where that came from." The inner rod of strength that had gotten her through the long hours of the night and the equally trying hours of the morning seemed to disappear.

She sagged against him. "Take me home, Ryan," she said softly. "Please, just take me home."

It was after noon by the time they got back to the bungalow. He helped Britta into the bedroom where she stripped to her bra and panties and got into bed.

"Ryan, please don't go," she said as he started to leave the oom. "Stay here with me," she said, her eyes already drowsy with the approach of sleep. "I know you're exhausted. You'll sleep better in the bed than on the sofa."

He was too tired to fight her, and the bed looked far too inviting. He shucked his jeans and pulled off his shirt, then crawled beneath the blankets next to her.

She cuddled against him, and that's all he knew.

He awoke several hours later and found himself staring into her amazing blue eyes. "Have you been awake long?" he asked.

"For a little while." A tiny frown danced between her brows. "I've been thinking."

He rose up on one elbow, grateful that their bodies weren't touching in any way. "Thinking about what?"

"That night he took me, while I was unconscious, why didn't he just tie me into the bow of a rowboat and drown me like he did Rebecca Johnson?"

"I don't know, Britta," he answered. "There's no way we can know the mind of the man responsible. Maybe he was experimenting with you, with the drug. It's possible if you didn't follow his command and drown yourself by walking into the sea, he intended to tie you to the bottom of a boat."

"Why would he dress us like that? With the gown and the seashell necklace? What could it mean?"

"It's obviously part of a ritual of sorts." He ran a finger down the side of her face, her skin baby soft. "You're trying to make sense of a madman. Until they catch him, until somebody can talk to him, we might never have the answers to those questions."

"It's over, isn't it?" she asked softly.

"It's over for us, but I have a feeling it's just beginning for the town of Raven's Cliff," he replied.

She rolled onto her back and stared up at the ceiling. "We won't be leaving here together, will we?" She didn't look at him.

The thick lump that formed in his throat surprised him. "No, we won't," he replied softly.

She closed her eyes and went back to sleep.

SHE AWOKE TWO HOURS LATER. She was alone in the bed, the cold pillow next to her letting her know Ryan had been gone for a while.

Ryan. She rolled onto her back and stared at the pattern of waning sunlight dancing on the ceiling. He was going to leave her again. After all they'd been through, after everything they had shared, he was going to walk away from her one final time.

The pain that pierced through her was unimaginable as she thought of moving on, of living her life without him. After all she'd already lost, her identity, her job, her friends and almost her very life, it seemed particularly cruel that she was going to lose him, too.

She couldn't fight his past. She had no tools. She couldn't go back and embrace the little boy he'd been, frightened by his parents' fights, hiding in a closet. It broke her heart. He broke her heart.

Wearily she got out of bed, driven by hunger and the need to spend what little time was left in Ryan's company. A glutton for punishment, she thought to herself, as she pulled on a pair of clean jeans and a T-shirt.

The minute she opened the bedroom door she realized she and Ryan weren't alone in the bungalow. She could hear the sound of Ryan's voice and another low, deep voice coming from the kitchen.

She stood just outside the door and closed her eyes. She

knew who was in the kitchen with Ryan. Her new keeper, the FBI agent who would take Ryan's place.

They were seated at the table, a large pizza in front of them. The new man had sandy blond hair and caramel colored eyes and as she entered the room he stood and offered her a friendly smile.

"Britta, this is Special Agent David Kincaid," Ryan said.

"Hello, Britta. Ryan has been catching me up on everything that's been going on. Sounds as if you've had a rough time."

She motioned for him to sit, then she took a seat at the table. "Yes, things have been difficult."

"Hungry?" Ryan pushed the pizza closer to her.

"No, thanks," she said. The hunger that had driven her from bed had disappeared the moment she saw the new man seated at the table. He was proof that her time with Ryan was over. She'd hoped for one more day. She'd hoped for one more night. "Are you from Boston, Agent Kincaid?" she asked.

"Please, call me David," he said. "And yes, Boston is home, although my wife is from the West Coast."

"So, what are the plans?" she asked, not looking at Ryan but rather keeping her gaze focused on David Kincaid. He looked like a nice man. Smile lines radiated out from the corners of his eyes and he seemed relaxed and open.

"Tomorrow we'll leave here and go back to Boston. We'll put you up in a motel for a couple of days until you can make a decision where you'd like to be relocated," David replied.

"Is it safe for me to return to Boston?"

"We'll make sure you're safe," David replied. "Although the way things are going with the Boston Gentlemen gang members we don't think there's a high risk to you, but for the couple of days we're there I'll be with you."

She nodded, then finally looked at Ryan. "And what about you?"

He held her gaze, and she saw his love for her there, shining from those warm green eyes of his, radiating across the table with the force of a physical caress. It was there only a moment, then gone, extinguished by a darkness that took its place.

"I'm already packed up. I'm going to take off in the next hour or so," he replied.

An hour or so, that's all she had left of him. It hurt so much. She felt as if her insides were being squeezed as hard as Kelly had squeezed her neck.

"Any news while I've been sleeping?" she asked, her voice huskier than usual. She cleared her throat and reached for a slice of the pizza.

"Chief Swanson called to check to make sure you were okay," Ryan said. "He's going to have his hands full. We know Rebecca Johnson was a victim five years ago and that you were almost a victim. Now he's going to have to investigate to see if there were any victims between those times. Because of the time span he's certain that whoever is responsible is a local."

Britta looked out the window where the purple haze of dusk was falling. In the distance the top of the lighthouse was visible. The lighthouse that hadn't been lit by Nicholas Sterling III on the night of the anniversary of the deaths of Captain Earl Raven's wife and children; the lighthouse where a curse had been born.

A serial killer on the streets, a mysterious fever sweeping the town and secrets lying just beneath the surface. She was ready to leave Raven's Cliff behind.

She'd been located here by a rogue FBI agent because he'd thought it would be easy to get to her in this sleepy fishing village. She'd survived a gang, a murderous FBI agent and a serial killer. But at the moment she felt as if she might not survive losing Ryan.

She wanted to weep, but there had been too many tears shed over the past couple of days. She was cried out. She took a bite of the pizza, but it tasted like cardboard. She laid it back down and got up from the table. "I'm sorry, I'm not feeling very well. I'm going to lie down for a little while longer."

Returning to the bedroom she blinked at the tears that burned in her eyes. She would pack, that's what she'd do.

She opened her suitcase and began to grab the things she'd hung in the closet. Action, she needed action to keep her mind off her pain. Keep moving, she told herself as she pulled clothes off hangers and piled them on the bed.

She'd cleared the closet when Ryan knocked on her door and peeked in. "I'll bet you can't wait to leave this place," he said as he came into the room and closed the door behind him.

She finished folding a sweater, placed it in the suitcase, then straightened and looked at him. "I'd rather be leaving here with you."

He jammed his hands in his pockets, a deep frown creasing his forehead. "David is a good man. I've worked with him before. If you want to get him talking, just ask him about his wife and kids. He'll keep you safe and see you settled some-place where you can build a new life."

"I want a life with you."

"Britta, please." Stark pain raced across his handsome features. "It's better this way."

"Better for who? For me? For you?" She took a step to-ward him. "Are you sure, Ryan? Are you sure you want to tell me goodbye again?" She wanted to grab him by the arm, wrap her arms around his neck and hold him close until he changed his mind.

"Someplace inside you there's a little boy who wants to believe in love, who wants to believe in a happily-ever-after. Let him out, for God's sake, let him out." She'd been wrong—she hadn't finished crying, for she was crying again, unable to stanch the tears that flowed down her cheeks.

He remained stoic, hands still shoved in his pockets and those beautiful eyes of his shuttered and closed off. "I just came in to tell you goodbye," he said.

And then he turned on his heel, walked out the door and closed it gently behind him.

She stared at the closed door for a long time, her tears continuing to fall. She moved back toward the bed and sat on the edge. She remembered this pain. This was the way she had felt the first time he walked away from her, from any idea of them together.

At the moment her heart hurt so badly she wasn't sure she'd survive the night. And yet she would. She'd survive, and tomorrow she'd be moved to a motel in Boston. She'd spend the next couple of days trying to decide what path to choose for her future.

Eventually she would be happy again. Maybe she'd find another special man and maybe she wouldn't, but she would find happiness.

She got up from the edge of the bed and moved to the window and peered out, where night shadows had begun to fall and fog had begun to form.

She'd find her happiness once again but she wasn't so sure about the people in Raven's Cliff. She turned away from the window at the knock on her door. "Yes?" she said.

"I just wanted to make sure you didn't need anything." David's voice called through the wood.

"No, thanks. I'm fine," she replied. A minute later she heard the faint tinny sound of the television coming from the living room.

She moved back to her suitcase and finished folding the last of her clothes, leaving out only what she would wear the next day when they left Raven's Cliff behind.

She could pick where she wanted to go, anyplace in the United States, and yet the only place she wanted to be was in Ryan's arms. She could pick what kind of job she had, a new name if she wanted it, but what the FBI couldn't give her was the man she loved.

Maybe she should just go to bed, she thought. Even though it was early and she'd had a nap, either the sleeplessness and the trauma of the night before or Ryan's abandonment had etched a deep weariness inside her.

She sat on the bed once again, her head filling with thoughts of Rebecca Johnson. Had Rebecca been the first victim of the serial killer who now walked the streets of Raven's Cliff? Had there been others?

She'd be leaving here with many questions. What was causing the illnesses? Would they ever find Camille Wells's body? Was the mayor on the take, and why had Britta verbally attacked him the way she had that day? Would Swanson be able to catch the serial killer before another young woman was cast into the sea?

So many questions and no answers, but it was easier to focus on all these things than it was to think about Ryan, to mourn for what might have been.

With a gasp of surprise she jumped up as her bedroom door burst open and Ryan stood there.

"Ryan, what are you doing here?" she asked. Her heart began to beat an unsteady rhythm at the sight of him.

"I forgot something," he replied. He stepped into the room and closed the door behind him.

"Where's David?" she asked.

"I told him to take a walk." Ryan stalked toward her, a determined glint in his eyes.

"What did you forget?"

"You."

She stared at him, afraid to believe, afraid to hope. She wanted to throw herself at him, grab hold of him and never let him go, but instead she remained rooted in place as he jammed his hands in his pockets and gazed at her with fiery eyes.

"I was halfway out of town, so sure that I'd made the right choice, that I was doing what was best for everyone involved by leaving you." He pulled his hands out of his pockets and tugged at his chin. "I love you, Britta."

The words swirled around inside her head, cascading warmth through her body. "I know you do," she replied softly. Again she fought the impulse to throw herself at him. But he hadn't committed to anything yet. Maybe he'd just come back to unburden his soul and the end result would be the same. She'd be left alone.

"It terrifies me," he said in a low voice.

She finally took a step toward him. "There's nothing to be afraid of," she said. "We love each other, Ryan. We've been through hell together and come out on the other side. We've lived together and we've fought together. And nobody called the cops, nobody threw a single punch or a dish. You had a wonderful role model on what an unhealthy relationship is all about. I challenge you to find anything in our relationship that is unhealthy."

He smiled then, a slow upward curve of those lips she loved. "Aah, Britta, you challenge me on every level."

In that smile, in the smolder of his eyes, she knew he wasn't going anywhere without her. Her heart soared as he reached out to her, and she flew into the embrace of his arms.

"I'm always going to be eleven years older than you," he said.

"That doesn't matter, there are times you act like an adolescent boy," she said teasingly.

He tightened his arms around her. "I can't believe how close I came to losing you forever. The thought of you in that boat shop, the terror you must have felt, the idea that you could have wound up like poor Rebecca Johnson drives me crazy."

"But I didn't," she replied. "I'm here and I'm safe and I'm ready to move on to my future with you."

"I want that, too, Britta. I'll relocate wherever you want to go. I can work out of a field office anywhere in the country."

"I'll be happy anywhere on earth but in this place," she replied. "In fact, I can't get out of this cursed town fast enough."

"As far as I'm concerned we can leave tonight…now. I've wasted enough time. I'm ready to start our future this minute. I'm planning on being your handler for the rest of your life, Britta," he said.

She smiled up at him. "Now, darlin', you know I'm a woman who refuses to be handled," she said in her best imitation of his Texas drawl.

He laughed, then lowered his mouth to hers and kissed her with all the tenderness, the passion and love she knew he possessed.

When the kiss ended she smiled up at him. "I remember we talked about kids once, about having them. I want that, Ryan. Someday I want to have your babies."

"I'd like that, and we'll make sure they speak not just English but two other languages, as well."

She looked up at him curiously. "Two languages?"

His eyes lit with a devilish gleam. "We'll teach them to speak Norwegian and Texan."

She laughed, then sobered. "We'll teach them one more language, as well." This time it was his turn to look at her curiously, and she smiled. "We'll teach them the language of love."

With those words he took her mouth again in a kiss that stole her breath and sealed her future.

The town of Raven's Cliff might be cursed, but at the moment Britta felt as if the curse that had been on her head had been lifted, banished by the shining light of Ryan's love.

THE FRONT DOOR to the faded yellow cottage slowly creaked outward. He looked first to the left then to the right, satisfied that the streets were deserted. It was after midnight and he didn't expect to meet anyone on his outing.

He carried only his car keys and one other item with him as he got into his car. The last thing he wanted was to be seen, and the cloudy night and deep shadows coupled with the ever-present thickening fog worked to his advantage.

It had been almost two weeks since the body had been pulled from its watery grave in the sea. DNA results had confirmed that the body was of Rebecca Johnson. Yesterday the town had mourned the woman who would have been one of its own if fate and a madman hadn't intervened.

Even though he hadn't been at the official ceremony, despite the fact that he had no contact with the townspeople, all he had to do was read the newspaper to know that everyone was on edge.

People were getting sick, and a serial killer walked the streets. The paper had run an article about Captain Earl Raven, complete with interviews by locals who had commented on the curse of the old man.

It didn't take him long to reach his final destination. He parked just outside the old iron gates that led to Raven's Cliff Cemetery. The cemetery was as old as the town and a popular tourist attraction for those who loved reading old headstones.

He grabbed the item that he'd brought with him from the passenger seat and left the car. The black clothing he'd worn allowed him to perfectly blend into the night as he walked the path toward the newest grave.

When he reached it he stared at the headstone visible in a sliver of moonlight that suddenly appeared. He knelt down and ran a hand over the lettering on the stone. Rebecca Johnson. The engraved name was followed by the years of her birth and her death.

He placed the white rose he'd brought with him gently on the grave, then stood and stared out in the direction of the sea, where the moonlight caught and glittered for a moment on the top of the Beacon Manor lighthouse. The light was there only a moment, then doused by the storm clouds gathering strength.

A storm was coming, a storm of mammoth proportions and he knew that when it was all over, the little town of Raven's Cliff would never be the same.

* * * * *

Things are just beginning to heat up as
The Curse of Raven's Cliff continues next month
with Jessica Andersen's
WITH THE M.D....AT THE ALTAR?,
only from Harlequin Intrigue!

THOROUGHBRED LEGACY
The stakes are high when it comes to love,
horse racing, family secrets
and broken promises.

A new exciting Harlequin continuity
series coming soon!
Led by New York Times
bestselling author Elizabeth Bevarly
FLIRTING WITH TROUBLE

Here's a preview!

THE DOOR CLOSED behind them, throwing them into darkness and leaving them utterly alone. And the next thing Daniel knew, he heard himself saying, "Marnie, I'm sorry about the way things turned out in Del Mar."

She said nothing at first, only strode across the room and stared out the window beside him. Although he couldn't see her well in the darkness—he still hadn't switched on a light... but then, neither had she—he imagined her expression was a little preoccupied, a little anxious, a little confused.

Finally, very softly, she said, "Are you?"

He nodded, then, worried she wouldn't be able to see the gesture, added, "Yeah. I am. I should have said goodbye to you."

"Yes, you should have."

Actually, he thought, there were a lot of things he should have done in Del Mar. He'd had *a lot* riding on the Pacific Classic, and even more on his entry, Little Joe, but after meeting Marnie, the Pacific Classic had been the last thing on Daniel's mind. His loss at Del Mar had pretty much ended his career before it had even begun, and he'd had to start all over again, rebuilding from nothing.

He simply had not then and did not now have room in his life for a woman as potent as Marnie Roberts. He was a

horseman first and foremost. From the time he was a school-
boy, he'd known what he wanted to do with his life—be the
best possible trainer he could be.

He had to make sure Marnie understood—and he understood, too—why things had ended the way they had eight
years ago. He just wished he could find the words to do that.
Hell, he wished he could find the *thoughts* to do that.

"You made me forget things, Marnie, things that I really
needed to remember. And that scared the hell out of me. Little
Joe should have won the Classic. He was by far the best horse
entered in that race. But I didn't give him the attention he
needed and deserved that week, because all I could think
about was you. Hell, when I woke up that morning, all I
wanted to do was lie there and look at you, and then wake you
up and make love to you again. If I hadn't left when I did—
the way I did—I might still be lying there in that bed with you,
thinking about nothing else."

"And would that be so terrible?" she asked.

"Of course not," he told her. "But that wasn't why I was in
Del Mar," he repeated. "I was in Del Mar to win a race. That
was my job. And my work was the most important thing to me."

She said nothing for a moment, only studied his face in the
darkness as if looking for the answer to a very important
question. Finally she asked, "And what's the most important
thing to you now, Daniel?"

Wasn't the answer to that obvious? "My work," he answered automatically.

She nodded slowly. "Of course," she said softly. "That is,
after all, what you do best."

Her comment, too, puzzled him. She made it sound as if
being good at what he did was a bad thing.

She bit her lip thoughtfully, her eyes fixed on his, glimmering in the scant moonlight that was filtering through the window. And damned if Daniel didn't find himself wanting to pull her into his arms and kiss her. But as much as it might have felt as if no time had passed since Del Mar, there were eight years between now and then. And eight years was a long time in the best of circumstances. For Daniel and Marnie, it was virtually a lifetime.

So Daniel turned and started for the door, then halted. He couldn't just walk away and leave things as they were, unsettled. He'd done that eight years ago and regretted it.

"It *was* good to see you again, Marnie," he said softly. And since he was being honest, he added, "I hope we see each other again."

She didn't say anything in response, only stood silhouetted against the window with her arms wrapped around her in a way that made him wonder whether she was doing it because she was cold, or if she just needed something—someone— to hold on to. In either case, Daniel understood. There was an emptiness clinging to him that he suspected would be there for a long time.

* * * * *

THOROUGHBRED LEGACY
coming soon wherever books are sold!

Thoroughbred Legacy

Launching in June 2008

A dramatic new 12-book continuity that embodies the American Dream.

Meet the Prestons, owners of Quest Stables, a successful horse-racing and breeding empire. But the lives, loves and reputations of this hardworking family are put at risk when a breeding scandal unfolds.

Flirting with Trouble

by *New York Times* bestselling author

ELIZABETH BEVARLY

Eight years ago, publicist Marnie Roberts spent seven days of bliss with Australian horse trainer Daniel Whittleson. But just as quickly, he disappeared. Now Marnie is heading to Australia to finally confront the man she's never been able to forget.

The stakes are high when it comes to love, horse racing, family secrets and broken promises.

A new exciting Harlequin continuity series coming soon!

REQUEST YOUR FREE BOOKS!

2 FREE NOVELS PLUS 2 FREE GIFTS!

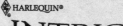

HARLEQUIN®
INTRIGUE®

Breathtaking Romantic Suspense

YES! Please send me 2 FREE Harlequin Intrigue® novels and my 2 FREE gifts (gifts are worth about $10). After receiving them, if I don't wish to receive any more books, I can return the shipping statement marked "cancel." If I don't cancel, I will receive 6 brand-new novels every month and be billed just $4.24 per book in the U.S. or $4.99 per book in Canada, plus 25¢ shipping and handling per book and applicable taxes, if any*. That's a savings of close to 15% off the cover price! I understand that accepting the 2 free books and gifts places me under no obligation to buy anything. I can always return a shipment and cancel at any time. Even if I never buy another book from Harlequin, the two free books and gifts are mine to keep forever.

182 HDN EEZ7 382 HDN EEZK

Name _____ (PLEASE PRINT) _____

Address _____ Apt. #

City _____ State/Prov. _____ Zip/Postal Code

Signature (if under 18, a parent or guardian must sign)

Mail to the **Harlequin Reader Service:**

IN U.S.A.: P.O. Box 1867, Buffalo, NY 14240-1867

IN CANADA: P.O. Box 609, Fort Erie, Ontario L2A 5X3

Not valid to current subscribers of Harlequin Intrigue books.

Want to try two free books from another line?

Call 1-800-873-8635 or visit www.morefreebooks.com.

* Terms and prices subject to change without notice. N.Y. residents add applicable sales tax. Canadian residents will be charged applicable provincial taxes and GST. This offer is limited to one order per household. All orders subject to approval. Credit or debit balances in a customer's account(s) may be offset by any other outstanding balance owed by or to the customer. Please allow 4 to 6 weeks for delivery. Offer available while quantities last.

Your Privacy: Harlequin is committed to protecting your privacy. Our Privacy Policy is available online at www.eHarlequin.com or upon request from the Reader Service. From time to time we make our lists of customers available to reputable third parties who may have a product or service of interest to you. If you would prefer we not share your name and address, please check here. ☐

HI08

Royal Seductions

Michelle Celmer delivers a powerful miniseries in
Royal Seductions; where two brothers fight for the
crown and discover love. In *The King's Convenient Bride*,
the king discovers his marriage of convenience to the
woman he's been promised to wed is turning all too
real. The playboy prince proposes a mock engagement
to defuse rumors circulating about him and restore
order to the kingdom…until his pretend fiancée
becomes pregnant in *The Illegitimate Prince's Baby*.

Look for

THE KING'S CONVENIENT BRIDE
&
THE ILLEGITIMATE PRINCE'S BABY

BY MICHELLE CELMER

Available in June 2008 wherever you buy books.

Always Powerful, Passionate and Provocative.

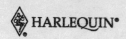

INTRIGUE

COMING NEXT MONTH

#1065 LOADED by Joanna Wayne
Four Brothers of Colts Run Cross
Oil impresario Matt Collingsworth couldn't abide his name being dragged through the mud. So when Shelly Lane insisted his family's huge Texas spread held devastating secrets, Matt was a gentleman all the way—and saved her from certain death.

#1066 UNDERCOVER COMMITMENT by Kathleen Long
The Body Hunters
Eileen Caldwell never imagined she'd walk into her past and find Kyle Landenburg waiting for her. The Body Hunter had saved her life once before—would history repeat?

#1067 STRANGERS IN THE NIGHT by Kerry Connor
Thriller
Bounty hunter Gideon Ross thought he could protect Allie Freeman, but he didn't even know her. In a game of survival, whoever keeps their secret the longest wins.

#1068 WITH THE M.D....AT THE ALTAR? by Jessica Andersen
The Curse of Raven's Cliff
When the town was hit with a mysterious epidemic, was Roxanne Peterson's only shot at survival a forced marriage to Dr. Luke Freeman?

#1069 THE HEART OF BRODY McQUADE by Mallory Kane
The Silver Star of Texas: Cantera Hills Investigation
People said the only thing Brody McQuade kept close to his heart was his gun. Was prominent attorney Victoria Kirkland the only one brave enough to poke holes in his defense?

#1070 PROTECTIVE INSTINCTS by Julie Miller
The Precinct: Brotherhood of the Badge
Detective Sawyer Kincaid had the best instincts in the department. And only by standing between Melissa Teague and danger could he keep this single mother safe from harm.

www.eHarlequin.com

HICNM0508R